WOLFSONG

Wolfsong

AMANDA PRANTERA

QUARTET BOOKS

First published in 2012 by
Quartet Books Limited
A member of the Namara Group
27 Goodge Street, London WIT 2LD

A catalogue record for this book
is available from the British Library

ISBN   978 0 7043 7246 7

Typeset by Antony Gray
Printed and bound in Great Britain by
T J International Ltd, Padstow, Cornwall

**FT
Pbk**

For Milou one day

But of all the games, the one I like best is pretending there is another Asterion.

Borges, *The House of Asterion*

1

It was Nico who first told me I was a werewolf. But then it was Nico who first told me almost everything. She was seated at her dressing table when she spoke, fiddling with the clasp of the magnificent topaz and diamond necklace she had chosen to wear that evening. Her back was turned towards me, but in the mirror I could see her eyes burning brighter than the jewels.

I could say nothing in reply. A lump had suddenly formed in my throat and I needed to swallow but couldn't because my mouth had gone dry.

'Oh go on, Sarah Whatever-your-name-is,' she teased. Stretching out a hand towards the bed, she snatched up a fur stole left there by one of her other guests and began stroking it rhythmically, twisting the pile into little tufts with a circular movement of her forefinger. 'Fur. Beloved texture. So much nicer than hair. Doesn't it say anything to you? I bet it does.'

I shook my head; the lump grew larger till it threatened to choke me.

Nico shook hers, and the matching topaz earrings swung like bells. 'I don't believe it,' she said in that drawly voice of hers, gracing the verb with an un-countable number of *e*'s. 'How old are you, for God's sake? You can't be that much younger than me, can you?'

Somehow, lump and all, I managed to inform her that I was nearly nineteen.

'Nearly nineteen? That years or days? No, seriously, you mean you've reached this far in your life without ever, not *ever*, I don't say realising but at least suspecting . . . ' The teasing tone came back, and she held the stole to her face, so that her eyes now glowed at me through the tufts. 'There must have been something, no? Think back, little she-wolf mine. Some outbreak or other. Trouble with a dog, maybe? That's a classic. Or with a bunny, or a hamster, or one of those scruffy little guinea pigs we used to be given as kids? Nix?'

My throat contracted again; I could only splutter.

She beckoned imperiously, 'Come here a sec.'

I moved towards her like a sleepwalker. She picked up a hand mirror and thrust it into my face. 'Close your eyes,' she said, 'and then open them quickly, wide. See that little film over your eyeball like a shutter? That's your double eyelid. Mine is the same, look. Only wolves have double eyelids. That's where we get them from, from our wolf genes.'

My head was reeling. Words were piling up behind the lump – protests, denials, or maybe confessions – but before I could utter them Nico suddenly got to her feet, whirled round, tossed the stole back onto the bed and flounced out of the room, catching me by the hand as she went and dragging me behind her. 'Oh forget it,' she said. 'I'm sorry I spoke.' It was hard to tell whether

her tone was apologetic or just impatient. 'It's party time, Sarah Whatsit, let's go party.'

* * *

My awakening. My second birth. My revelation or apocalypse or whatever. In the normal way of things Nico and I would never have met. I knew who she was, of course, from my scanning of glossy magazines. I knew she had just turned twenty-one, because her coming of age party in January had received ample coverage in all these publications, and I knew that for the occasion her husband had made her a present of a sundial and a fruit-eating bear. And I knew she was a marchioness, because her title was always much in evidence too, and I knew she was alleged to be one of the fastest swinging elements of swinging London by those responsible for measuring such oscillations, and I knew she was beautiful because not even the worst photos – of her yawning at a wedding, or sulking in a night club, or pulling faces at the photographer at a film premiere on the arm of Ringo Starr – could disguise the fact.

But I also knew, or thought I did, that I was not in her social league and didn't wish to be. In fact, had my mother not been present when the invitation arrived, I might have thrown it away, thinking it a joke, or else a mistake on the part of the organisers of the dance for which Nico's dinner party was being given. (I still think this last may have been the case, and if so my thanks go to those inept organisers.)

My mum was adamant I should accept. A titled person above the rank of baronet could never do wrong in her eyes. This was not snobbery: it was an article of her religious creed that not even a recent spate of high-life scandals had managed to shake; she had merely upped her cut to peers and over. (I wonder, incidentally, if she would be so adamant now? And I wonder, when all is over, if she will try to preserve her faith by upping the cut again to dukes?) My collocation in the world had been a problem to her and my father, proportional to my growth. By this time it was so unwieldy it had begun to defeat them. With a last flicker of energy they had recently enrolled me in a secretarial college. I think my mum may have had dreams of me finding employment and marrying my boss, but my father had got to the stage when, regarding my future, he only had nightmares. This freak invitation extended, in their view, a last little thread of hope. It would have been churlish to disappoint them, so, in a cousin's ill fitting ball gown, with my hair backcombed into a loofah, off I went, flustered and late because of desperate last minute alterations to the dress.

From Nico's mind-shattering words in the bedroom onwards, I was too taken up with my own thoughts to notice much of what happened around me on that otherwise memorable evening. Forgivable, I reckon: it is not every day that you change species. Up to that moment, though, I took careful note of everything. I was quite practised at this. Being so shy and awkward it was one of the few things I felt happy doing when in company of people I didn't know: just sitting there quietly and observing, hoping no one was observing me.

The house Nico lived in when in London – Sherwood House, town abode of her husband's family since Regency times – was extremely grand and extremely shabby, a combination that seemed to me to cancel very nicely both defects. Stuccoed ceilings, chandeliers, brocaded walls hung with ancestral portraits thick as stamps in an album – it reminded me of a huge iced wedding cake that the mice had got at. The hall I entered was high and chilly and paved in black and white chequered marble, and on one side of it stood a model ivory temple as large as a summerhouse, and on the other a broken down bicycle. The fruit-eating bear was no longer in residence – I heard during dinner that it had been shipped back in disgrace post-haste to where it came from – but signs of its brief run of anarchy were rife. My coat was placed on the bicycle crossbar by a butler attired in a morning coat over a pair of jeans. There was a fair pile of coats there already.

'You've cut it fine, Missy,' he said. 'I can hear them moving in to din-dins already. Come on, I'll take you up.'

The first floor dining room he ushered me into was fortunately warmer than the downstairs regions, but you couldn't say the same for my reception from the people assembled there, waiting for their hostess to allocate them their seats. True, Nico gave a little start when she saw me, but it was not a reassuring gesture,

13

not at this stage. Still less reassuring was the fact that she had to check on the piece of paper in her hand to discover my name, and only half of it at that.

'Ah, now we can eat,' she said with a note of severity, and made a brusque circling movement of her arm like a sower scattering corn. 'This is Sarah, everyone. Sarah, this is everyone.' She went on to name each individual, but coquettishly, making it clear that it was more for their benefit than mine. 'William, my sweet and perfect husband' (bestowing a kiss on William's anything but sweet and perfect jib sail of a nose). 'Our dearest friends Lucy and Edward' (airborne kisses for both, whom I recognised from my magazines as a top model and her actor husband). 'Our dearest *unmarried* friends Jake, Tristram and Raymond' (fond little pout of lips for each). 'And . . . ' (pause to scan vainly the scrap of paper now scrunched into an illegible ball) 'and . . . um . . . these two charming girls here whom I'm sure you know already.'

Had I not fallen under her spell the moment I set eyes on her I would have found this display obnoxious: here are we two young married beauties, top of the Olympus, was what it effectively said; here are our Zeuses beside us; here a bit further down are three young demigods, officially invited for you but actually ours also, so don't go getting ideas; and there at the foot are you three little mortals. Admire and keep your mouths shut.

I had no difficulty doing either: I was bewitched. We sat down to eat at an oval table, our host and hostess facing one another at each end, with a fellow deity to their right and a demigod in close proximity. This made for two main areas of conversation, each of which could link themselves effortlessly across the divide that was me. The two girls on the opposite side constituted more of a block, and the young man sitting between them – I don't know which he was, I had muddled their names already – was occasionally obliged to address one of them in order to relieve his solitude, or else to speak rather loudly across her, or simply tuck in to his food. His behaviour didn't seem to ruffle the girls at all: they were debutantes doing the season, like professional cricketers their minds were on the ball to come. Over, or rather under, the flow of godly conversation they sent messages to one another via signs and whispers; for them the dinner was just something to be sat through before play could commence.

I might have envied them their self-containment had I too not been perfectly content to be ignored by my semi-divine neighbours. My only fear was that the isolated third might suddenly raise his head and talk to me across the table, but thankfully this never happened.

It's meant to be boring, listening to conversation about people you don't know. I found it fascinating. The names for a start. There were some, like Raymond itself, that I'd never thought possible could belong to posh owners, and those in question were as posh as they come; there were others, mostly nicknames, that I would have thought no owner, posh or otherwise, would have been able to endure, and then there were the ones that stood outside the range of criticism: the Tempests and the Atlantas and the Strongbows, about whose owners I could form no opinion whatsoever: you didn't own names like that, they owned you.

The actual subject under discussion I found less interesting to begin with: it was little more than a list of who, amongst this batch of names, had been seen by whom during the past week and where and doing what, and inquiries about who was going where at the coming weekend and in what houses they were going to stay. The houses too had quite arresting names and were referred to as individuals, mostly in a disparaging way. Taddon is always gloomy. Rawby's so grim. Cordwick is impossible. Pensworth needs going over with a gigantic sponge. But as the wine-level in the glasses sank, the level of interest rose.

I couldn't quite make out what the 'grass' was they now began talking about so merrily, but I knew from the way they shot glances at me and the debutantes that it was something adult and forbidden, probably some mild form of drug. I could also see that William, the Marquess, though it was he who was telling the story, was not entirely happy about its implications and was airing it more in a spirit of exorcism than genuine mirth. What had happened apparently was this. A few days earlier he and Nico and a group of friends, most of them Nico's, had been going to some music festival, to be held in the open air. Over dinner, sitting round the table much as we were now, he had asked innocently, wondering whether his clothes were

16

right for the occasion ahead, 'What's the score tonight, are we sitting on the grass?' At which not one but two of those present had immediately reached into their pockets with cries of 'No, no, no, for goodness sake, there's plenty, help yourself!' And they had placed packets of this shady commodity, whatever it was, on the table.

This anecdote was greeted by uproarious laughter, even from the two debs who I doubt had been listening to a word. I laughed along so as not to seem stuffy, but I was more taken up by watching all the faces and trying to spot what was going on behind the laughter. People don't realise it, but laughter is often a very faulty screen. I caught a slight glimpse of pain on the face of the teller, slight bafflement on the debs', open admiration on all three male guests', and on the Lucy creature's peach-bloom cheek I noted an ugly little pleat of satisfaction, indicating she would secretly have welcomed her dearest friend's social disgrace. Only on Nico's did I read nothing but amusement. Every part of her shone – her skin, her hair, her lips, her eyes, the precious stones adorning her, the ivory satin bodice of her dress.

She said later that I gawped at her at this point, which is probably true, and that that was why she started gawping back: in self defence. According to her, this was the moment she first looked at me properly and immediately recognized me for what I was.

This accelerated version is more romantic, but in reality I think it took her longer to twig. After giving that almost imperceptible start when I entered the dining room, which I think was in annoyance at my late arrival, not in recognition, I can't remember her looking at me in the least bit attentively until the meal was well advanced, let alone gawping. Round about pudding time, however, I suddenly felt her eyes on me and began wondering in panic if something had gone wrong with my hairdo, or if the hectically cobbled stitches round my waist had split.

She focussed on me in spurts, it was most disconcerting. She would throw back her head, laughing at some other anecdote – anecdotes had accompanied us through the entire meal, I had never heard so many at one sitting – and from under her lashes I would see this beam of scrutiny abruptly swivelling towards me. Or she would turn to her left hand neighbour, seemingly listening to something he was saying, and all the while her eyes would be darting past him in little sorties, attempting to catch mine. This went on until we filed out into the drawing room for coffee when, more disconcerting still, I actually felt her breath on my neck in passing and heard her make a kind of sniffing sound. By that time I had decided either she must be mad, or else something had gone terribly wrong with my toilette. Her suggestion that perhaps I'd like to go upstairs to the loo before going on to the dance inclined me to the second hypothesis, her footsteps and the hurried swirl of her skirts on the stairs behind me, to the first. I doubt I would have guessed the real reason for her interest had I lived to be a hundred, which now of course I never shall.

2

When I got home that night I was outwardly still quite neat and tidy, with my long white gloves unsullied and my shantung shoes unscuffed, so I conclude I must have spent very little time at the dance, if any. But inwardly I was in utter turmoil.

Instead of undressing for bed straight away I sat in front of my mirror in my borrowed finery, seeing Nico's face in place of mine and feeling her words scrape through my head like a harrow through a field. Or, closer to the mark, like a dredger through a muddy pond. Bringing to the surface slimy clusters of things that had long lain buried.

Scenes. Pictures. Memories. Some from so far back they had no words attached to them, only mouths opening and shutting, others replete with captions, others trailing whole chunks of dialogue in their wake. The one with the earliest feel to it was perhaps the scariest. I saw the wooden rungs of a bed, painted powder blue – a child's bed therefore, my childhood bed – and through the rungs the face of a young woman peering. A vaguely familiar face, perhaps that of a stopgap nursemaid engaged for my nanny's hols. Her mouth was open in a Munch-like scream and her skin

19

was ashen, but whatever noise she was about to make was stifled by a hand which suddenly appeared from nowhere and clamped itself over her jaw, yanking her away. In the background there was a soothing, hissing noise, but I had the impression it was not meant for me.

Another early picture came in a navy blue frame – presumably the borders of the hood of the pram out of which I was looking. In the foreground were my short stubby legs, encased in yellow woollen gaiters, strewn over by a wreckage of fur particles and kapok, and in the centre of the frame, staring straight at me and filling it almost entirely, stood a strange woman in a flowered overall, with a headscarf on her head, tied in a bow at the top to cover a row of tight little curlers which peeked out like so many accusatory metal fingers. The front ones were actually shaking loose with indignation.

'Look what that child did!'

The answering voice was calm, placating, it came from behind the pram, it might have been my mother's, though she was never much of a pram pusher. 'It was only a toy, Mrs Tilbrook.'

'I know, but look what she did to it. Little horror. Little heathen. I'd learn her some manners, smart, if she was mine.'

'Oh, come on, she's only a toddler.'

'Rum toddler,' said the strange woman with a shudder. 'Never seen such a thing, not in all my born days.'

The other voice was no longer so calm. It was tinged

with anxiety now, plus a little trill of hectic amusement. So, yes, it definitely was my mother's: humour was always her refuge. 'Why, what did she do exactly? I was window shopping, I didn't see.'

The woman's hand reached out and prodded gingerly at the kapok. 'That's what she did. But it's not so much the *what* as the *how*. And now if you'll excuse me I'll be off home for a glass of something, I need to steady my nerves.'

These two scenes, for all their colours, came to me through a kind of red filter that lent them a hot, uncomfortable atmosphere and whose origin I was presently unable to establish. Not that I had much time for reflection, with the speed at which the dredger was now working.

This reddish haze was anyway on a wane. Next to surface was a still in which I could see my father standing in the hallway of our house holding a shredded mink coat in his hands and showing it to – or perhaps trying to conceal it from – an enraged lady in a black dress, presumably the coat's owner. In the foreground, like a detail from a painting by Veronese, skulked my mother's corgi Rebecca, her hindquarters bunched under her as if she had just received a kick. This image, kicked dog, irate female and all, was bright and luminous and only faintly pink, almost as if the filter were now shading into gold.

Another picture, with a still brighter aura to it, was simply a whirl of small beige-coloured flakes, almost totally obscuring my vision as I scrabbled for some desired object hidden beneath them. Had it not been accompanied by an audio memory of my nanny's agitated voice describing to my parents a mishap at a children's party to which she had just accompanied me, I would have had difficulty placing it, but by running the two memories together I managed fairly easily to identify the flakes as belonging to a bran tub. More than that I could not deduce, but the memory for some reason was a fond one and it made me smile. Or made Nico's face, superimposed on mine in the mirror, smile.

Clearest and most brilliant of all, however, was a far more recent scene, dating from my twelfth year when I had been sent away to boarding school. Quite what my parents' reasons were for taking this, in retrospect, rather risky step, I have never fathomed: maybe they wanted me to socialize, maybe they could find no more private governesses willing teach me, or maybe, poor things, they simply needed a break. Anyway, whatever their reasons, off they packed me to this institution – for what mercifully turned out to be a very short stay.

In my conscious mind I had scores of memories of the place, nearly all of them filed away under the letter H for Hell. Me standing in the hall on arrival and being surrounded by a posse of girls in uniform and immediately classified as foreign. As prey, therefore, as legitimate quarry. Me donning the uniform they wore, trying to join them, blend with them, and failing. Me as an outsider trying to woo them and failing. Me trying to protect myself against them and failing. Me trying in vain to hide my misery from them, trying to laugh things off in the daytime and stifle the sound of my sobbing at night. Me trying to learn my persecutors' lexicon so that at least I could foretell what new torment was in store for me. And failing, failing, failing all along the line. What was a Twister? What was a Soaker? What was a Chinese Stew? Suspense increased my suffering to agony level, as was intended. The only new word whose meaning I managed to decipher, and pretty quickly at that, was Dormitory: it meant a torture chamber.

Curious, therefore, that this last scene with the exhilarating, champagney flavour to it should have been located right there, in the dormitory. Or not? No, I decided; with Nico's shimmering reflection there to cast new light on things, not curious at all. There it was, the long narrow room with the two bow windows at the far end, separated by a high dressing table, and there stood the two symmetrical rows of beds along either wall, covered by bright tartan coverlets under each of which lay an enemy. And there was I, their victim, in the bed closest to the door, crying silently, waiting for a signal from the ringleader to indicate that it was sufficiently quiet and dark for my nightly ordeal to commence. On this particular night the name of the game was Around the World. Its rules had just this moment been explained to me with relish. On pain of forfeits so terrible that they had not yet been explained, merely alluded to by another menacing series of names, I was to make my way round the entire room, starting from my own bed and back again, without my feet ever touching the ground. Woe to me if they did. Woe to me if I slipped or cheated or refused to make the trip. Direst woe of all if I sneaked: another girl had done that once; she had regretted the move bitterly, they had seen to that.

Looking at the beds, at the heavy wooden cornice over the door and the sturdy cupboard beside it, and calculating the distances, I could see that the two long walls and my end of the room were all negotiable – just. I could hurl myself at the door and hope for a hand-hold; then, using arm-strength alone, I could edge my way along the cornice, get up some swing when I came to the end of it and grasp out for the top corner of the cupboard. The cupboard had carved rims round its doors and also at key-level – these would provide footholds, or toe-holds at the very least. As I traversed I could rest my arms at bit, get my strength back for the next swing, which hopefully would land me on the bed opposite mine. Unless an occupant deliberately tripped me (a hazard I must allow for and guard against), the next part was simple: I merely had to leap from bed to bed down the entire row. And the same applied to the return journey. The big problem, I could see, lay at the far end, where the two gaps between window recesses and dressing table were so wide that they couldn't possibly be bridged by the method of swinging. Even if there had been something to swing on – curtains, for instance, or cords – which there was not. As I hesitated, racking my brains for a solution, there came a ghoulish whisper from a neighbouring bed: 'The last new girl,' it said, 'tried crossing the hard part *outside* the windows. She fell and bust a leg and was expelled.'

The memory, so detailed up to this point, suddenly became a little blurred. Several images flashed before my eyes, but in such quick succession that I had trouble separating them. The various pieces of furniture I had been measuring and assessing seemed to rush at me all together. One minute I was dangling from the cornice of the door, my fingertips aching with the effort of trying to work up a pendulum motion without letting go, and the next, with quite a different feeling in my fingers, as if they were shorter now, and scratchier, and the whole of my body was much more powerful, I was bounding across the very top of the cupboard and swooping down onto the first tartan blanket, and then the next and the next and the next, and then onto the cushion of one window seat and then with a huge leap, scarcely brushing the surface of the dressing table as I went, onto the cushion of the second. Then another leap – joyous, springy, I could have done twenty such, no, a hundred – and then more beds and beds, and finally back to mine. All this seemed to have taken place in utter silence; accompanying my clear round there were no sound memories at all, but in the ensuing hush I could clearly recall wriggling quickly back into bed and lying there and hearing the sound of someone crying, and noting with relief that it wasn't me.

In the mirror was my own face now. I did the blinking trick that Nico had recommended, and sure enough there was the membrane: my hallmark, my second lid. I was too tired to think coherently, to line up the data and draw the inferences that I knew needed drawing, but it didn't seem to matter. Nothing seemed to matter. The knowledge was there; acknowledgement could come later. As I dismantled the loofah, gently combing the wodge of matted hair back into orderly strands, I felt a great sense of peace settle on me. For the first time in my nearly nineteen years of muddled existence I had an inkling of what I was.

3

The journey that I made that night of the ball, Nico herself had made seven years earlier in almost total solitude. Aged fourteen, on a train in the French Riviera, she had been apprised of her condition by a stranger sitting opposite her. A stranger in the usual sense but kindred in the less usual. He had not been very sympathetic about it either, from the sound of it. Speaking French, very fast and with a thick southern accent she had found it difficult to pierce, he had told her the bleak facts of what he assured her from experience would be her very bleak life: loneliness, incomprehension, the status of a pariah – these were the things that awaited her and with which she would have to learn to deal. *Tristement pour elle.* When, speaking in a whisper so as not to wake the adult who was accompanying her, Nico had put forward a timid question about the moon and its influence, he had at first affected not to hear, then when pressed he had merely hunched his shoulders in typical Gallic fashion and muttered: in these things there were no rules, she would just have to work it out for herself. 'Are there many of us?' she had asked next. Fortunately not, he had replied with a fastidious sniff, fortunately the con-

27

dition was rare – *extrèmement rare* – and had gone back to his newspaper. He left the train soon afterwards, at Nice, without offering further information or advice, beyond handing her a scribbled address on a torn off piece of rail ticket. A London address – she thought she might still have it somewhere. When she had asked him what it was for he had finally given her a look with some compassion in it and had said: when the time came she would know what it was for. She had never felt the least inclination to pursue the matter, so either the time the man spoke of had not yet come or else he'd been talking through his Basque beret. By now, whoever had lived at the address had probably moved on anyway.

We were in Nico's bedroom again when she told me all this. We seemed to live there nowadays: it was the ideal place for talking and we had so much to talk about. As we exchanged memories, which were often so painful, we could pursue other pastimes that were not: drag out clothes from the cupboards and try them on, for instance, or sift through the many heirlooms in Nico's jewel case, spilling them out onto the bedspread and picking at them like magpies. Tonight William was away on business, the evening was ours entirely, and while listening to Nico I was experimenting with the set of topazes and diamonds that I had first seen her wearing. The stones didn't suit me as well as they did her, I was too dark for topazes, but they were still my favourite.

Weeks had passed since our first meeting – weeks

that felt like days, they had flown so quickly, but that felt like years from the depth our friendship had reached. Officially I was still living with my parents and attending the typing school, but to all practical purposes I had moved into Sherwood House and become part of its grand and lackadaisical ménage. After the dinner party I had written Nico a short letter of thanks, saying rather bluntly that I was more grateful for what I called her 'eye-opening advice' than anything else, and she had immediately contacted me. I was flattered by her haste, not yet realising that inside the huge ring of friends and hangers-on that surrounded her like a nimbus, she was every bit as lonely as I was. I had gone round to see her at lunchtime; at dinner time we were still talking. That night – what little remained of it – I had slept in a guest room, into which I had since moved so many of my things, one by one as I needed them, that it had gradually become mine. For the time being the arrangement suited all of us well: Nico and me because we had each other, William because he looked on me as a safer type of friend for Nico than the grass-bearers, and my parents because not only was I absent, *Deo gratias*, but they could explain away my absence to one another in comforting terms: 'Our Cinderella daughter has finally met her prince at the ball'. That my prince was in fact a mutant marchioness was a detail easily overlooked: their years of guardianship had turned them into pros at over-looking.

'That's a poison ring you're wearing,' Nico was now

saying. 'It's Italian; it's very, very old. Look, this is how it worked.' She touched a spot on the side of the diamond surround, and the topaz centre suddenly flipped open revealing a little gold cavity within. 'You kept a powder inside there, and when your victim wasn't looking, toof! You slipped the powder into his wine.'

'Or her wine,' I prompted. I was trying to school Nico in feminism but it bored her, as did everything ending in 'ism', or so she claimed.

'Yes, or her wine,' she conceded. 'But I think men made better victims, they probably drank more. Faster too, so they didn't notice the taste.' She clicked the little case shut again and covered my hand for a brief moment with hers. 'Females are just as poison-worthy as males, of course they are, you ninny, but they are more restrained.'

I looked at the centre stone of the ring with new interest. So clear and yet with all that murky history behind it. 'How long, do you suppose, since somebody used it?'

Nico pulled a grimace. 'Only a couple of years,' she said. 'My mother in law used to use it. She used to fill it with Eno's Fruit Salts and sprinkle the stuff into people's drinks; it was her idea of a joke.'

I hadn't yet met William's mother, who lived in a wing of the ancestral home in Devon since her husband's death and rarely visited London, but I knew that her relationship with Nico was not an easy one. It could hardly have been otherwise: William was rich and titled and hardworking and exceptionally sweet natured; in social terms, and not only, he was a prize. His mother had probably counted on him marrying an equally dear, kind, well-bred and well-heeled Lady Geraldine Gruesome Gore or someone. A girl with faultless manners, faultless background and a faultless complexion. An old fashioned English rose. Instead he had chosen Nico who, even if you didn't know she was a hybrid, was still a bit of a let-down for an exacting parent in law. Immoderately beautiful, no money of her own, a polo playing rake of a father, dead at forty, a mother, evidently with a penchant for the genre, who had run off with another polo player and presently lived with a third in Brazil – no, Nico made a great showing in the press, but she was definitely not possessed of the sterling qualities that a dowager marchioness would require in a bride for her only son. Dollar qualities might have made up for the lack but there were none of those either, and certainly no Cruzado: the only thing her mother had ever brought her from Brazil, according to Nico, being a bag of unset gemstones as a wedding present. With a wry smile: 'She was always tuned in to my needs.'

Late into the night, in the big double bed, whispering like children, we continued our confessions. When I was through with my memories I found myself telling Nico, almost without meaning to, about the coloured haze that shrouded them. For some reason I hadn't liked to broach this subject yet, but under cover of darkness it was suddenly easy.

31

She listened without interrupting, her body very still. 'The red film is shame, of course, you know that already,' she told me when I had finished. Her voice was sad. 'I used to feel it too. It's like falling into a huge red inkpot – you think you'll never get rid of the stain.'

I received this in silence. She was right, it was shame and I had known so all along. And it still burned.

'And in a way I suppose you never do get rid of it,' she went on, echoing my thoughts. 'But then comes the gold and covers it up.'

'What is the gold then?' I asked her. 'Is it pride, or what?'

I felt her nod very gently, just stirring the pillow. 'Yes,' she whispered. 'The gold is pride; it's the other face of shame. They go together: you couldn't feel shame if you didn't feel pride. Pride in what you are. Pride in what you do if you do it well. Even if it's . . . ' Her voice tapered so that I could hardly hear it, 'if it's . . . you know . . . well, you know . . . '

I found this explanation a bit evasive. It was not so much the unfinished phrase – even on my slender experience with fur coats and toy rabbits I had no difficulty finishing that myself – as the unfinished idea behind it. 'But why should the guilt be the first side to show itself?' I asked. 'Where does the guilt come in?'

With a lightning twist she rounded on me, pinning me down on the mattress with her weight. 'It's . . . not . . . guilt, stupid!' she hissed, pushing me deeper into the springs with each word. 'Never say it's guilt; never say it's wrong – that's the trap they try to lure us into. What's wrong with us? There's nothing wrong. Where does the guilt come in? It doesn't. Shame comes in, but shame . . . Ouff!' She rolled back to her own side of the bed. 'Shame is different.'

'Different how? Different in what way?'

'I don't know,' she said. 'I know nothing about guilt – how can I when I've never felt it? Maybe it's heavier than shame, that's what, or maybe . . . Anyway it's different because it makes you feel guilty, and shame just makes you feel ashamed.'

'That's circular,' I said. I was tempted to say tautologous but I feared it would just make her laugh. My vocabulary often did, it made William laugh too. 'That's a circular argument.'

Even this seemed to amuse her. 'Circular?' she whispered, drawing a ring round my nose with her finger, 'So what. Everything worth its salt is circular. The sun is circular, the moon is circular, the world is circular, so is that old topaz ring you admire so much, so are these pesky pearls which have somehow got in here and are digging into my bum. There!' And so saying she yanked out the errant pearl necklace and threw it into the darkness where it landed with a clatter.

'So is the cell,' I added. This fact struck me as being somehow significant.

'The cell? What cell? Oh, I see,' she said, 'a science cell, I thought you meant a prison. Yes, so it is. And I'll tell you something else . . . ' She snuggled up beside me, drawing her knees to her chin. 'So is a wolf as it sleeps.

33

And now shut your muzzle, dearest Sarah, because it's four o'clock in the morning.'

A wolf, cushioned on the rug of its own pelt, nose tucked into tail – yes, a sleeping wolf was circular too. And that too for some reason struck me as being significant. A circle was a safe but isolated shape: perhaps I had meant a prison after all?

4

In order to last, the ties of friendship need sealing with some nice sticky substance. And the best product for this purpose – perhaps the only product, if you consider carefully – is one of the four cardinal bodily fluids: sweat, secretion, tears or blood. Toil binds, sex binds, sorrow binds and so does a shared deed of violence. Provided, of course, the friendship is there in the first place.

Nico and I were idle as sloths; when we were in bed together we just talked or slept; we had nothing to cry over, not yet at any rate, and although our wolf streak might make us blood-hungry at times, we were never bloodthirsty – only humans are that; it looked therefore as if we would just have to dispense with the glue and hope for the best. But then came our visit to Delham, and the seal was set.

Delham Castle was William's family home. Like their town residence it had come to the Sherwoods in Regency times when their comparatively recent fortune had been made. (In the rag trade, William always added modestly whenever the subject was raised: big-scale rags but rags all the same.) The façade and show parts of the house were therefore of that date, but to the rear of them, like crumbling molars behind a set of flashy front dentures, lay parts of the original fortress to which the building owed its name.

In one of these parts, suitably renovated with chintz and an Aga and double glazing, its tiny garden protected from the gaze of public visitors by a complex arrangement of fences and awnings somewhat nautical in character, lived Lydia, Marchioness of Sherwood, William's mother. Our present visit was in fact in response to a direct summons on her part: an American travel magazine was doing an article on the pottery factory she had recently set up in the coach house as a money spinner, and she wanted Nico to pose for the photographers.

Nico had agreed, but only after William had begged her to do so for his sake. Technically, I suppose, Delham was her home as well as William's, but from the way she talked about it during our journey there – rather like her guests at that first dinner party, with intimacy and disparagement combined – I gathered that her stake in the place was small and that it was the elder woman who was the real lady of the house.

Now came a suggestion that confirmed me in this opinion. 'Sarah's into paintings and stuff,' Nico announced to William as we left the car. 'She wants to visit the house properly. I'm going to buy tickets for the two of us and just go round like everyone else. What do you think? Will we have time before the photographers get here?'

'Oh for God's sake don't be so silly,' William scolded

her hastily. 'It would embarrass Miss Franklin no end. Nico, you really have no idea of people's feelings. You'd put her in a ghastly position, poor woman, she'd think you were checking on her or else taking the piss. There are pictures of you all over the place too. It would make for awkwardness all round.'

Nico was unconvinced. 'I don't see why. Nobody would notice. And Miss Franklin could do with some checking anyway. Last time we were here I heard her proclaiming that the fireplace was designed by a member of the Addams family. Maybe she had Morticia in mind.'

No smile from William. He looked pained. 'Please, Nico, no. Mummy would hate it if you did a thing like that.'

There is always something odd about a grown man calling his mother Mummy. To her face I suppose it's allowable, but when talking about her to other people it has a subservient ring. Justified in William's case because if not under his mother's thumb exactly he was under her big toe, ball of foot and heel, to be trampled on at her caprice.

I realised this as soon as I saw them together. No, even before I saw them together: I realised it the moment Lady Sherwood senior emerged from a small gate to the side of the house and began walking towards us across the flagstones, basket of beheaded roses on her arm and Labrador in tow. I saw the power of her stride and the strain that it put on the seams of her corduroy skirt, and I saw William's shoulders droop forwards slightly as if someone had put a weight on them, and I needed no further sign.

In William's defence I must admit the Dowager Marchioness was indeed an awesome woman. When Churchill placed such faith in the British populace's capacity to withstand German invasion, she must have been one of the stalwart prototypes he had in mind. I had no difficulty imagining her standing at the gate of her grounds whirling a spade and lopping off heads with it, in fact I had difficulty imagining her doing much else. Her virtues – courage, I presume, to give her her due, plus steadfastness, energy and a healthy lack of imagination – were those proper to a warrior society. The Age of Chivalry, the Age of Enlightenment, the Victorian era with its bourgeois morality and scientific bent, all these had passed her by untouched, she was a far more ancient product. She would have had much in common with Bodicea. Her unwitting arrogance quite took your breath away. She had married into this family of what I am sure she regarded as pushy Georgian drapers in order to move with the times and stay put at the top level of society where she rightfully belonged, but the roots of her own family tree reached much deeper into the soil, giving her the unshakable poise of an oak. How the gentle William could have sprung from those puissant loins was a mystery. Not than he would have sprung, either, he wouldn't have dared, he would more likely have slipped out stealthily and started heading for freedom, only to be scooped up and enfolded in the equally powerful maternal embrace.

From which, to see him now, trotting obediently into it again like a five-year-old, he had never since totally escaped.

I sketch Lady Sherwood (I hate calling her by that name: it shouldn't belong to her at all) as a caricature, but unfortunately she wasn't. There was no diminishing her awfulness by laughter, she was much too strong and real and individual. She was also rather pretty – in the face at any rate – and prettiness fits ill with ridicule. Nico got round the problem by switching off entirely in her presence and hardly ever mentioning her in her absence. Which is why I knew virtually nothing about the woman save her propensity for practical jokes. That she was a human steamroller I'd had no idea, but was beginning to form one quickly.

'Mmn, who is this 'ere?' She inquired loudly in an assumed cockney accent, disentangling herself from her son with a gesture of impatience and bearing down on me, flanked by her dog.

The Labrador's hackles were raised. Had its owner possessed hackles these would have been raised also. Lady Sherwood was an earthy woman, close in touch with nature, and I think her nose had already told her I was not of her kind in any sense of the word. I imagine she had already formed the same opinion of Nico and in the same manner.

'This is Sarah,' Nico told her levelly, conceding nothing.

'Sarah, eh?' A grubby, diamond-bedecked hand stretched out and tugged at mine forcefully, almost pulling me off balance. 'Sarah what? Sarah who?' Then, straight away, before any answer could be proffered, 'Who's her father? Do I know him? What does he do?'

Nico shook her head vaguely and made no reply. I was already, after a mere handful of seconds, beginning to understand her attitude of total closure towards her mother in law: with a person like this you could cross swords, kiss the knout, pass under the yoke, throw down the gauntlet, do all sorts of old fashioned power-connected things, but you couldn't enter into everyday social commerce at all.

I too remained silent. It was left to William to furnish the information as best he could. 'Um . . . Sarah's father is an um . . . a barrister, I think,' he said with an apologetic glance at both me and his mother, but at his mother first. 'Isn't he, Sarah? Or a solicitor. I forget which. A lawyer anyway.' He gave an uneasy laugh and tipped his nose towards the ground, putting me in mind of an ostrich seeking cover. 'A man of the law.'

'A solicitor,' I confirmed, taking pity on him.

'A solicitor,' Lady Sherwood echoed. 'Is he now?'

Even had this been intended as a question, which it clearly was not, there would have been no way of answering it. And anyway it was addressed, not to any of us but to the dog, which was still standing there by its mistress's side glowering, its upper lip puckered into a snarl.

The animal appeared to take courage from this brief interchange and began edging towards me in an un-mistakably hostile manner until Lady Sherwood caught it by its collar and restrained it. She set down her flower basket, squatted so that her head was on a level with the dog's and then butted it severely three times on the forehead with her own. I counted the clunks. 'Bad, bad, bad,' she told it, chuckling. 'You're a bad Eddie and you must stop that straight away.'

She looked up and her eyes met mine: they were radiant with a pleasure she did not bother to conceal. 'I *do* apologise for him,' she said. It was quite the emptiest apology I had ever heard. 'His party manners are appalling. Because he's so beautiful' – this said with a sideways glance at Nico – 'he thinks he can get away with anything.' Her forehead inclined towards the dog's again, making gentler contact this time. 'Don't you, you spoilt old jealous softie? Who's going to Crufts this year, eh, and who's going to win all the prizes?'

'Eddie is Lydia's passion,' Nico announced in a flat, expressionless voice. 'Eddie and gardening.' I don't know how she did it but in these few words she some-how managed to convey the fact that Lady Sherwood had no other passion, either for her son or for anyone else.

The elder woman looked up sharply, rose to her feet and glanced with a heavily exaggerated gesture at her watch. This was evidently the way she and Nico did their sparring – through obliqueness and silences and little darts whizzing around in the ether, visible only to an attentive eye. 'Oh dear,' she said briskly, 'The enemy encroaches. Sad news for you two girls: I'm going to have to spirit William away from you. We have a boring business meeting with trustees and people. You can join us for lunch if you like – though that'll be deadly boring too – or if you'd rather you can chicken out and do your own thing. I'm sure Mrs Woodruff, if you ask her nicely, would be only too happy to fix you sandwiches. Then we can have a lovely cosy get-together later over dinner.'

Nico dealt with this dart very dextrously, I thought. The poker face she had worn so far flooded with manifest relief. 'That's sweet of you, Lydia,' she exclaimed. 'What could be nicer? Chicken out and chicken sandwiches. But we won't bother Woody, we'll go and have them in the pub instead.'

'Pub ones are filthy,' said Lady Sherwood with a shrug. She knew when she was bested. 'But suit your-selves. As long as you're back before the photographer and crew arrive.'

'What time are they due?' William asked in the silence that followed, sounding just like a theatre prompter.

His mother shrugged again and rounded on her heels, manoeuvring the Labrador on the same radius and giving it a hefty shove to send it on its way. 'How should I know?' She said, her voice dwindling in volume as she followed the dog towards the house. 'I told them firmly, 'After luncheon', that was all. I didn't want them barging in on us late morning and then wanting to be fed, people are so thoughtless that way. Say two or thereabouts. Basket!' She called out over her shoulder more loudly.

I thought the command was meant for the dog until I

saw William stoop and retrieve the gardening trug and hurry off in his mother's wake.

The rest of the day was fortunately more relaxing. Until sundown at any rate. Nico and I had lunch in the nearby pub and I basked in her reflected glory. The innkeeper treated us as if we were film stars and royalty and long lost relatives wrapped into one. He called Nico 'Your Lovely Ladyship' and me 'Kiddo' which I though struck rather a nice balance, fed us like Strasbourg geese, and categorically refused payment. We came away feeling very special, at least I did; this kind of thing had probably palled on Nico by now.

The photographer didn't show up till four, and the business lunch was evidently a protracted affair because there was no sign of William either when we got back. For two whole hours we wandered on our own through the grounds, Nico pointing out to me all her favourite spots. But in a detached sort of way, as if the place had nothing to do with her and these features she professed to like so much had been learned off a map. We visited the Orangery, the Herb Garden, the Water Garden and the Wild Garden that lay behind; we sat by the lake in the shade of a willow and took off our stockings and dabbled our feet in the water and chewed bubble gum we had been given at the pub. And every time we heard a party of sightseers approach we hid and giggled. Only then did I feel that Nico had been here often and was familiar with the layout: she knew the hiding places.

While she was busy being photographed I took the

official guided tour round the house with Miss Franklin, who showed far more pride of ownership than Nico did. 'This is our second Marquess, painted on his return from the Grand Tour. No, the canvas is not damaged: he caught smallpox in Naples. This is our famous green library; the colour was chosen to match the Marchioness's eyes. There she is on the other side of the fireplace, she must have been quite a character. To match the *eyes*; I said the *eyes*, not the teeth.' This is our this, this is our that. When she got to a recent portrait of Nico my heart nearly missed a beat. If anyone had made a quip about this sitter I would have hit them over the head with my guide book. But no one did, they just stared at the canvas in stunned silence, and some of the old biddy visitors made clucking noises.

'Our present Marchioness,' said Miss Franklin, preening.

I felt as proud as she did. When the tour ended she took me confidentially by the elbow and escorted me to a concealed door at the end of a long passage. 'Lady Sherwood said you were to go this way,' she whispered. 'It's a short cut. Go across the lawn there, past the fountain, then follow the path between the yew hedges and it'll lead you to straight to her private residence where you're having dinner. There's a little green door with 'Private' written on it, you can't miss it.'

Did William's mother lay this trap for me deliberately? Was it one of her practical jokes? If so the laugh was not on me, not the last one anyway.

I thanked Miss Franklin politely and off I set. The

tour had been a thorough one and dusk was already falling. As I approached the fountain I felt, with that radar part of me that seems to work independently of all the rest, a sense of danger. I could hear nothing, see nothing, smell nothing to base it on, but I knew the danger was there. Half way down the narrow, yew-lined path I realised what it was. It was Eddie, the Labrador. I heard his growl, deep and threatening, and then I saw his head, low on the ground in ambush position, peeking out between the trunks of the yews.

I stopped and began to backtrack. This was a mistake because he rose and started slinking towards me, growling louder, so then I changed tactics and stood still and confronted him. I tried to make reassuring doggy noises but they came out quite different from what I intended and only made things worse. He came closer, gathering speed. In the twilight his teeth glinted like serrated knife blades, and his eyes were two little red embers. It crossed my mind to shout for help but I feared the noise would only spur him to attack. It was touch and go by now: one false move and he would spring. I held my ground and gradually he slowed down again and came to a slavering halt about a yard from where I stood.

In this position of deadlock we eyed each other for what seemed a long time, but was probably only a minute or so by the clock. An elastic, endless minute. Reason told me to keep absolutely motionless and wait until someone came looking for me, which sooner or later they were bound to do, but annoyingly and mysteriously some faculty other than reason seemed to be in command. When Eddie's ears finally lowered a fraction in sign of relaxation and he granted himself a first blink, instead of altering my own facial expression to match I felt my jaw contract and heard a strange grating noise issue from my throat. Immediately the space between the dog's ears shrank again and he began to bunch his other muscles as well. Bad sign, I thought in panic, bad sign; your fault, you fool, keep quiet, don't move.

All might still have been well, I might still have been able to restore the balance, had not – at that very moment – a bat suddenly swooped down, almost brushing my hair in passing. This tipped the scales, and very fast. I ducked, lost my footing slightly and took a fatal step backwards; Eddie, encouraged, bounded forward with teeth bared and made a great grab at me, catching, luckily, only the hem of my skirt in his jaws. I swirled away from him to a noise of ripping material and then, rather similar to what had happened to me that night in the school dormitory, my vision suddenly went blurred. (Interference of the second eyelid, said Nico, and she could have been right.) Dizziness set in and my last clear thought was that I was about to faint. I heard a howl, unearthly, spine chilling, and my perspective changed: I saw things lower down, all muddled up together: grass, gravel, branches, a flash of metal from the tag on Eddie's collar, and the soft pale folds of the skin of his throat and underbelly.

Then everything went dark. When I came to my senses again I was lying on the path in a very strange position, my legs folded under me, my arms stretched out in front like a Sphinx, and Nico was bending over me, shaking me by the shoulder. Or where my shoulder should have been but felt as if it wasn't. There was a funny salty taste in my mouth and when I wiped my lips with the back of my hand to cleanse them it came away coated with little short hairs.

For some reason that wasn't clear to me – but then nothing was very clear as yet – we were both of us out badly of breath.

Nico's face wore an anxious look. 'You OK?' She panted. 'Nothing broken? Nothing torn except for that?' And she pointed at my skirt which was truly in tatters.

I staggered to my feet and felt myself all over. My body seemed odd – numb and unfamiliar – but was apparently quite unharmed. 'I'm fine,' I said. 'Why? What happened? Did I fall, or what?'

Nico put her head on one side. She too, apart from her eyes, looked faintly unfamiliar. 'Don't you remember?'

'A bit,' I said cautiously. My memory was gradually coming back: it was not a comfortable process at all. 'I remember walking down this path and seeing that vile dog lying in wait for me under the trees. Eddie or whatever he's called. I tried to calm him down, I think, but he went for me, and then I must have fallen and banged my head . . . Or, no, perhaps it was the other way round, perhaps I tripped and fell, and then he went for me. Anyway, we had a clash. Where is he now, the beast? I don't want him coming back and . . . '

Nico made a funny sound halfway between a bark and a laugh. 'He won't be coming back, not for a while,' she said. 'We chased him right down the drive and out onto the road. Bravery is not his forte, poor Eddie, I should think he's still running.' She took a deep breath and stretched her arms above her head. 'God, we're unfit, the pair of us. We'll have to take more exercise in future. I'm blowing like a porpoise and so are you.'

'*We* chased him down the drive? You and I did?' I had no memory of doing that at all.

'Yup,' said Nico carelessly as if it was the most natural thing in the world.

'How come we did it together? How come you were here?'

'Because you called for me,' she said. Then after a moment's reflection, 'Howled for me, if you really want to know. Luckily I was in the bathroom changing, so I didn't have to explain anything to anyone, I just came rushing. And luckily when I got here that moron dog was savaging just your skirt and not the rest of you.'

My skirt. Fuddled though I was, I immediately realised that my skirt might act as a giveaway unless I did something to it, and quickly. I picked up the trailing material and started tugging at it, trying to remove the torn bits. By the time I had got the hemline roughly level it was very short indeed. Minis were coming into fashion but they were still considered very daring.

'Shit,' I said to Nico, 'I've only made things worse.

48

What is your mother in law going to think if I show up for dinner like this?'

Nico laughed – a proper full-blown laugh this time. She was evidently finding the situation very funny. 'If things go the way I think,' she said, 'Lydia won't pay much attention to your appearance. It'll be totally overshadowed by Eddie's.'

Oh dear, the Labrador was a horrid creature and deserved no sympathy from me, but even so I didn't like to feel responsible for having done it violence. The taste on my tongue and the mouthful of hairs didn't bode too well on this score. I was almost afraid to ask my next question. 'We . . . we didn't hurt him, did we?'

At this Nico's glee got the better of her entirely. She bent down and retrieved a small cylinder shaped object from the gravel where it had been lying and began brandishing it in the air, hopping from leg to leg in a kind of Red Indian war dance. 'Hurt him, no,' she chortled, 'but damaged him, yes. Take a look at what you were chomping on just now. Take a look at the trophy you brought back from the chase in your jaws. Oh brother, who's going to Crufts this year and who's going to win all the prizes?'

She tossed the object towards me and then bent double with laughter. It was the tip, just the tip, the last three gristly vertebrae or so, of Eddie's pedigree tail.

5

Faust's wager was that he would never in his lifetime feel so happy as to say, 'Stop, Time, this moment is so beautiful I want it to last', and that if he did he would forfeit his soul to the devil.

Had I been Faust I would have lost my bet and soul on several occasions, all of them post-Nico, but never so finally as on the drive back to London that night of Eddie's comeuppance. When I close my double eyelids on this earthly parade, that is the picture I want to have before them: me and Nico on the back seat of the mini, bowling through the darkness side by side, singing 'How much is that doggie in the window, The one with the waggley tail?' And laughing ourselves nuts. And William from behind the wheel throwing back his head in jubilation and filling in the 'Woof, woofs'.

I'm not sure if William knew the real reason for our merriment. I was never sure how much he knew about anything where Nico and I were concerned. Sometimes I thought, everything; sometimes, not a lot. The business of the fruit-eating bear, for example: did he make the mistake of thinking that the animal was a member of the bear family, and that as such Nico might possibly take to it and vice versa, or did he just make a mistake, full stop? Such matters are delicate, and somehow, even when I could have done so, I never liked to ask. But anyway, whatever the extent of his knowledge it was enough to enable him to share in the fun of that evening and prevent him from asking questions. In certain ways he and I were very similar: we loved Nico without reserve, we loved being with her, and therefore we almost loved each other for keeping hold of her – insofar as this was feasible – through the tethers of our love. Certainly we were neither of us ever jealous of each other, and certainly we both ranked fairly low in the natural ranking order, I being – what would a zoologist classify me as? A kappa female? Let's say lambda to be sure – and William, for all his wealth and title, being more of a sigma male getting on for tau.

Did either of us realise that that evening was to mark a watershed? That something irreversible had happened and that never again would we resume the tranquil rhythm of our London *ménage à trois*? William had past experience to go by, he may have read the signals already. I had none, so that the bored, restless Nico of the following morning, groaning over her coffee and stretching out a hand towards the telephone in search of outside stimulus, came as a something of a shock.

But a shock I had to adapt to if I was to remain close to her, that I realised straight away.

'Annabel?' (Julian? Lucy? Peter? Polly? Paulie? Alexander? Mark? The lot.) 'It's me, Nico. Yes, I know,

51

foul of me, but I've been sort of . . . Yeah, you know how it is. Anyway now I'm back. What's up? What's on? A circus party? What, in the ring with the sawdust? Ah, I see. Where's everyone meeting? No, I hate El Cubano. See you at Grey's then later, say half past nine?'

See you, see you. In the phase we now entered we didn't see that many people – at least I didn't, I was generally too wuzzy – but we met hundreds. Jostled with hundreds. Danced with them, drank with them, argued with them, in some cases stayed with them in their houses, and span around in cars with them at breakneck speed to meet yet more. We went on a permanent amusement blind that lasted right up to summer. Most of my recollections from the period are of dressing: the short gap between waking up with a hangover in the late afternoon and issuing shakily forth into the evening on our stilettos being the only time Nico and I were ever totally sober. And even then we sometimes preferred not to be, and swigged tumblers of corrective vodka in our bath. Looking back I consequently see little apart from a jumble of laddered stockings and frothy, grimy petticoats, and badly crumpled dresses that we are trying either to iron or remove stains from, but without much success. We treat our clothes like rotten mothers do their children: with a corrosive mixture of disregard and passion. Sometimes the scars they bear are the only means we have of retracing what we've been up to while wearing them. Mud on a hem, grease in a pocket, broken down heels, sprinklings of wine or face-powder or strawberry juice on a skirt, and flashes of the previous evening come back to us.

'God, those fish and chips were a mistake, I can still feel them churning.'

'Was it Oxford we landed up at?'

'Must have been. Henry was there. He was the one who handed round the purple hearts.'

'Purple hearts mean purple farts. God. How did we get back? Did someone drive us, or did we catch the milk train?'

'Smells like train.'

'Yeah, smells like train. This too, take a whiff.'

'Train. There's a ticket in my bag.'

'What's this rent? Looks like I've been duelling.'

'You snagged that on the gate, remember?'

'Ah, yes, the college gate. So I did. Lucky I didn't rip my arse.'

Our weekend binges, being longer, sometimes printed memories with more substance to them. I can recall, for example, a whole group of us turning up at one of the most beautiful houses I have ever seen: a Palladian palace whose proportions on their own were enough to stun you, even before you noticed the delicate rose of the brickwork glowing between the honey-coloured fluting of the columns as if the whole building was blushing. Perhaps it was blushing too: blushing for us. Which member of the group it belonged to, I don't recall. I have a feeling it was the home of someone's elder sister who was away staying somewhere else. She must have got a nasty shock when she got back.

Although, no, the splendour of the place on this occasion cast a feeling of awe over us and kept us a bit in check. Which is probably why my head remained clearer and the pictures in it likewise. I can see myself being sick rather tidily into a lapis lazuli vase and rinsing it out the day afterwards. Never normally would I have done that – the rinsing, I mean. I can see Nico, clasped tightly in the arms of someone who isn't William, swaying to the strains of Bach's concerto for two violins as if it were dance music, and then abruptly kicking off her shoes and remaining barefoot so as not to ruin the parquet floor. The furniture was swathed in dustsheets; we didn't remove a single one, not even from the beds, just sprawled out to sleep on top of them and heaped clothes on ourselves to keep warm. We stubbed our cigarettes out in a huge Chinese vase filled with potpourri. Nico and I may have gone a bit over the top at some point, although not badly, because the second morning I recall Julian, known as Gloom, eyeing us blearily from the next door bed and starting to tell us his dream, in which we had apparently figured prominently, and then suddenly plucking something off his tattered overcoat and holding it up to the light for examination, and paling and saying no more. Except for, in slight stupefaction: 'You two are weird, aren't you? I mean you're really, *really* weird.'

William followed our rakish progress from the sidelines, perplexed and powerless: an adult whose charges are whirling round on the roundabout and who has no means of recovering them until the mechanism comes to a halt.

Which, luckily for us, following the unmarked but nevertheless strictly observed tempos of the London season, it finally did. The weather grew warmer, the parties grew fewer, London grew stuffier and the venues shifted farther and farther afield: outskirts, Home Counties, finally Scotland and abroad.

Invitations to everywhere and everything drifted through the Sherwood House letter box like tired migrating birds. Most of them remained there on the floor unheeded until swept up by a cleaning lady and delivered to Stewart, the be-jeaned butler, whom Nico and I suspected of selling them to tourists. Now and again William, on return from work, would open a couple and push them enticingly towards Nico's plate during dinner. Who knows, a change of air might snap her out of it. 'Lola's asking us to stay for Goodwood. They've got a horse in one of the big races. Pierre and Mimi are giving a dance in their château for their niece – the one that wanted to be a nun, remember? Could be fun, no? No? No, I suppose not, no.'

The only time I saw Nico at all positive about any of these suggestions was over a letter from some Scottish grandee buddy of William's asking him and her – and me by default – to go deer stalking. But here it was William who put the damper on. One look at Nico's thrown back head and dreamy expression as she rolled the word 'deer' around in her mouth, and he crumpled the letter and stuffed it hastily into his pocket. 'No,

Scotland's off this year,' he said, unusually firm for him. 'We need to get some sun. You look like wraiths, the pair of you.'

We did. Nico especially. In the few sane intervals when my brain was working clearly I was quite worried about her, but instinct told me to keep my worry to myself. Any suspicion of my turning from accomplice into keeper, and a fracture would form in our friend-ship, ready to widen into a split the moment it came under pressure.

Without that telephone call from Clarissa, I don't know where we might have landed up. Anywhere really. The downward spiral Nico seemed so intent on pursuing was getting steeper every day. Every night. The parties we attended were getting seedier and seedier. We took taxis to areas of London we'd never heard of, and often had great difficulty finding a driver willing to come and pick us up for the return ride. Gloom, who was about the only member of our earlier entourage whom the summer recess hadn't yet swallowed, on one occasion swore he'd found a fresh human placenta floating in one of the loos. He was joking, but the mere fact that he could do so with a chance of being believed, shows the kind of scene we'd got ourselves into: still high society, technically speaking, but with the 'high' no longer referring to the class altitude of its members, just the state they were in.

Then one evening, while Nico and I were soaking in our preparatory marinade of Floris and vodka, this friend of hers – this Clarissa whom I had not yet met –

rang from Italy to ask us to stay for the Spoleto festival, and that was it. In the space of a few minutes everything changed, and instead of sallying forth towards perdition we found ourselves intently poring over maps with William, picking at a telly supper and trying to discover where Spoleto was vis à vis the town of Collalto which was apparently where Clarissa's newly acquired house was located.

'Odd place to choose to go and live,' William said in genuine puzzlement. For a moment he sounded just like his mum: habitable Italy to Lady Sherwood would almost certainly have meant Tuscany full stop, and only very choice parts of that. 'It's all mountains from the looks of things. And the roads are all just little wiggly worms in yellow and white. No red ones at all. What's got into Clarissa? She fallen for a bandit or something?'

Nico looked up at him in surprise. 'You know sometimes, Will,' she said, 'you are positively psychic. Or did she tell you herself when you picked up the receiver? '

William blinked. 'What? You mean . . . ?'

They spluttered into each other's faces. I loved it when they were companionable like this. No, I was never jealous of William: we occupied quite different places in Nico's heart. 'He's not a bandit exactly,' Nico went on to clarify. 'The line was rotten, but from what I could gather he's a down at heel Neapolitan nobleman who's in some financial crack-up or other. He's signed some papers he shouldn't have done, and now he stands to lose his monogrammed shirt, so he's put all his spare cash in Clarissa's name and she's bought this house with it, which is miles from anywhere, and they're going to hole up there and lie low till everything blows over. Meanwhile they want some company. Ollie's there already, and they've got this Contessa coming – the one that was in the fellatio scandal with the Swiss Guard, remember, Willikins? You loved reading about that. Oh let's go join them, *do* let's.'

The pleading note was put there as a gift. A little sop to William's ego to create the illusion that the decision rested with him. 'We-ell . . . ' he said doubtfully. I could see him mentally weighing up the pros and cons: get Nico out of her sleazy London round and into fresh air and sunlight, all right, *but*, flip side: a foreign country, a remote spot, a scatty hostess, a louche-sounding house party, and if not deer, then probably plenty of other hoofed fauna just as troublesome – it might be out of the frying pan and into the fire. 'Thing is, if they've just moved in and have no readies to do it up with, the house could be hideously uncomfortable.'

Nico stroked him fondly down the bridge of his nose. Quite a risky operation, given its shape. 'They're not *that* broke, silly. Clarissa said Whatshisname . . . Leopoldo has managed to salvage a Guido Reni from the bailiffs and has stashed it away in the cellar – that should cushion them for a while.'

The Sherwood estate boasted several such cushions in the form of Rembrandts, van Dycks, Gainsboroughs, Constables and even an attributed Giorgione. 'Oh, piccies,' intoned William respectfully, 'Where would we all be without our piccies?' It was the sort of remark

I once would have puked at, but now simply found in character and rather sweet.

6

I had only been abroad twice before, to Brittany and Ireland. Three times if you count Wales. In none of these places had I encountered, on a gloves-off basis, the sun – and I'm talking woolly gloves here, as well as boxing. My first thought on landing at Rome airport, walking down the gangway and placing my foot on Italian soil, was that some nearby engine was running and I was standing in full blast of the exhaust. When I realised the heat was for keeps I had a moment's despair. I would never be able to bear it.

A hired car had been sent to collect us. It was just Nico and me for the time being – William was following on in a week. We clambered in, and it was like popping ourselves into a pre-heated oven: our skins stuck to our clothes and the clothes stuck to the seats, and as it drew away the car itself seemed to stick to the tarmac and only to progress with effort, its tyres slowly tearing themselves away from the molten substance beneath. There was some kind of football match on, or had been, and the road from the airport was clogged with hooting Fiats from whose roofs and windows sprouted highly coloured flags, with highly coloured people inside waving them. It was bedlam.

Nico, who had been to school in Florence at one point of her switchback school career, said something to the driver and he gabbled back a long rigmarole in which the word 'caldo' featured prominently. I took it to mean cold, and the sense of having stepped into a madhouse intensified. If this was cold in the opinion of an inhabitant, what was hot going to be like?

As their conversation developed – which it did fast, maybe a bit *too* fast for Nico's liking, because later I heard her emit a warning signal that ended it abruptly – I sank back in my corner and prepared to expire. Then, gradually, almost imperceptibly at first, the situation began to improve: the traffic thinned, the horns quietened, the sun sank lower in the sky and the car began to climb – out of the scalding brass dust bowl of the plains and into shaded woodland. I duly postponed expiry, and an hour or so later, when we reached the little hill town of Collalto with its castle and church and cascade of higgledy-piggledy houses, and its narrow streets almost obstructed by the gaggles of old men sitting out at tables playing cards and swigging wine, I archived the idea altogether. This was a place the fairy godmothers had visited en masse and lost their gift-filled luggage in. Not only would it not kill me, I could live on willingly. I was hungry by now, so in theory one of my senses should have felt deprived, but if it did the other four made up for it by rejoicing. Cool, soft, sun-drenched air on my skin; in my ears the ringing of bells and the crying of swifts; a spectrum of lusterware colours for my eyes, fanning through copper to amethyst to deep moss green and back again; and in my nostrils the mingled smells of wood smoke, beeswax, resin and broom, bound together by a strong underlying whiff of home cured ham.

Nico, even more than I did perhaps, set great store by smells and was clever at distinguishing them – one trait at least that her mother in law might have approved of, had she known. The movement of the car as it swung through a gateway and over a cattle grid threw us close together and I could feel her ribs expanding as she relished the bouquet of aromas, breathing it all in. (Could she already have sensed that other key component in the mixture, I wonder? No, not possible: the hills were not high enough yet and it was still farming land. And I don't think it was the smell that was finally responsible, anyway, I think it was the sound.)

'Nearly there now, Sarie. You're OK aren't you? Not regretting having come?'

I could only shake my head in answer: words seemed stuffy, dry little things all of a sudden, quite incapable of holding their own against this barrage of sensation.

Nico understood perfectly: she smiled and crinkled her nose at me and said nothing more until, almost half a mile of steep, winding, oak-lined avenue later, we finally came in sight of the house: a squat, square, pinkish stone farmhouse with one or two touches of grandeur, such as a crest of arms set into a small pediment over the entrance, and a semicircular flanking of cypress trees on either side. Then, 'Pool!' She hissed at me excitedly, pointing to a flash of turquoise between the trunks. (The driver jumped at the sound and nearly drove the car off the road: poor man, Nico's warning signal must have unsteadied his nerves.) 'Clarissa didn't say there was a pool. Wonder how it got there? Can they have hocked the old Guido Reni already?'

The mysteries of upper class solvency. When the members of other classes go broke they do just that: they break, with all the pain and trauma a fracture involves. The top layer no, its members just bend a while *pour mieux sauter*. I don't know if Clarissa and her Poldo, or Leo as he preferred to be called but rarely was, were still in the flexing phase or whether they were already bouncing back on the springs of their Mannerist cushion, but whichever it was, they were not going to allow it to affect the tenor of their lives one jot. Nor that of ours, their guests'. It was without doubt one of the comfiest, smoothest run houses I had visited since meeting up with Nico and William, if not *the* comfiest. In the English homes we had stayed in, however grand, however stately, the motor of the household, primed by its various drivers and attendants, had always been visible, audible, a factor to be taken into account, even when it was working properly, which it often wasn't. 'Um. Let's not sit too long over dinner tonight, if you don't mind. It's Saturday, and Robbins has his favourite sports programme . . . ', 'Um. We breakfast in here, everybody, and not in the main dining room any more. It makes it easier all round . . . ', 'Um. The garden is not looking *quite* its best at present: Don's daughter is getting married, so he's a bit taken up with . . . ' Um. Um. Um. Even Lady Sherwood senior had shown areas of rare sensitivity in her pachyderm casing where employees were concerned. Dear Mrs Woodruff, could you possibly do this? Dear Miss Franklin could you very sweetly do the other?

Here, in contrast, the motor just ran, with no noticeable rattles in the chain of command whatsoever. In fact you couldn't even see the chain. Beds were made, rooms were tidied, delicious meals were regularly laid out on the terrace, ready for consumption whenever we felt like it, the pool was cleaned, the garden weeded, and the most you would catch sight of would be the strings of an apron whisking through a doorway, or a figure in the middle distance wielding a broom or watering with a hosepipe.

When Nico, rather envious on account of the glaring contrast to Stewart, asked Clarissa how all this seamless efficiency was achieved she admitted she didn't really know. She had no say in the matter. The staff had come with the house, and after the sale had just gone on doing what they'd been doing before – probably for centuries. They showed no interest in their new employers' concerns and invited none in theirs in return. 'Perhaps if we hadn't been foreigners it might have been different, but seeing that we are . . . '

'Poldo's not a foreigner, surely,' Nico objected.

But Clarissa soon put her right. 'Yes he is – in these parts. In fact as a Neapolitan he's probably the most foreign of us all. *Inglesi* the locals had contact with, in the war and things. *Napoletani*, southerners, *meridionali* – might as well be Zulus for all that is known of their ways here in Collalto. Isn't that so, *amore*?'

Poldo, her *amore*, assented, as he assented to most things coming from Clarissa – requests, opinions, or even the somewhat startling pronouncements she was prone to make at mealtimes, a challenging expression on her face as if daring her listeners to disagree. 'In Nepal the wheel has not yet been invented.' 'That could easily be so, my love.' 'During the last ice age the world changed rotation and started spinning the other way.' 'Did it now? That is *curioso* indeed.' He and she made a surprisingly cosy and stable pair. From what little I had heard about them beforehand I had been expecting fastness and looseness on a fairly dramatic scale. In fact I was even slightly scared of what life in their company might be like. English abandon I could cope with: people just drank themselves legless and I along with them; but what would Italian abandon entail? Not even a viewing of La Dolce Vita in London before we left had prepared me for that. Spaghetti alla mescalina? Pompeian style orgies? Wine flowing from fountains? The Contessa publicly displaying the talent for which she had become famous?

Nothing of all this, it emerged in the sunny and relaxed days that followed. The Contessa – Arianna by name – was an elegant, rather withdrawn and demure lady of forty odd summers. And I say summers because clearly they, not the winters, were the seasons that besieged her brow. It could be she was going through

65

a chastened phase after all the hubbub, but in the weeks we spent together the only excess I ever saw her indulge in was sunbathing – an activity, or better, passivity, which she carried out with such dedication that by the end of our stay her skin was as dark and bronzed as the leather of the pumps I used to wear to dancing school. Her English, when she used it, was flat but flawless with no trace of slang or accent whatsoever: you could imagine her having learnt it in a school for interpreters, located in some linguistically germ-free spot like Pitcairn or the Falklands. She spoke little, however, in any language, and her facial mimicry and carriage were similarly unrevealing. As I say, poor woman, this might have been a belated manoeuvre designed to compensate for having been splashed in photographs over every scandal sheet in Europe and hailed as the new Messalina, Salomé and Jezebel rolled into one, but if so it was unavailing. Tolstoy once described a childhood game he used to play with his siblings where the rule was to stand in a corner and *not* to think of a polar bear. I don't know about the other members of our party, whether they all had the same trouble, or if it was just me and Nico and Ollie, but for us it was like that with Arianna. Every time we looked at her, or so we confessed to one another one tipsy evening as we sat out by the floodlit pool among the bats and fireflies, we would try so hard not to think of her engaged in some bit of oral naughtiness that the effort was self-defeating.

Ollie. Otherwise known, for his fresh soap-and-water complexion so fiercely at odds with his alcohol intake, as Bath Oliver. Ollie I had met before – at almost every party Nico and I had ever been to. He was one of those mysterious figures who, without ever dispensing hospitality, or thanking for it, or being or doing anything noticeable to deserve it, reaped it from every quarter. His presence constituted a hallmark, a guarantee of 'in'-ness, 'with it'-ness, and I suppose that was his secret. If hesitant guests saw Ollie across the threshold, or heard his aggressively languid voice raised in an extravaganza that at another time or place might have earned him a lynching, that was enough – they knew they could participate in the gathering without risk of seeming dowdy or ill informed.

A creative job like any other creative job: long hours, hard work, and constant reinvention – in his case of the self. Here in Italy, though, Ollie seemed to regard himself as off duty and spent no care whatsoever on the upkeep of his persona. The carapace of the hard drinking, fast thinking salon intellectual peeled away under the rays of the Umbrian sun to expose a kindly, serious minded young man with middle class aspirations, a bent towards hypochondria, and a fiercely loving Russian mum who bombarded him with telephone calls, and about whom he was unswervingly loyal even though, to judge from the sounds that reached us through the receiver, the temptation to use her as copy must have been great. No bitchy brilliance, not even at mealtimes, no rapier repartee, just a nice easy-going playmate you could talk to about everything under the sun. With a preference for just that: the tiny *hic et nunc* happenings in our lazy pool-lizard existence.

We read detective novels, thumbed through them with our sun-oiled fingers and criticized the plots. People came to swim and eat, and after they had gone we criticized them. A trifle less desultorily. Taking tips from Arianna that involved bits of sticking plaster and deep commitment, we bronzed rebel bits of our anatomies, like inner thighs and armpits and the little white half moons that lurk under the buttocks, to achieve the most fantastic, homogeneous tans. We swam; we drank litres of Pimm's and watered-down Chianti and little else. Now and again, in the cool of the evening, the more energetic of us would go for a stroll under the holm oaks accompanied by Clarissa's dogs. She had a whole pack of them that, like the staff, had come with the house: they were fat, friendly, low-strung creatures, totally unbothered by Nico and myself. In this we were lucky: it's always a bit of a toss up with dogs: either they fear and loathe you at first sight, like Eddie did, or else they fail to notice you almost, so familiar do they find you.

Although perhaps more than luck, it was election. The dogs, after all, had chosen to remain in this place under the new ownership, and if I had been offered the option I would have done the same. If someone had told me I had been born there or had lived there in another life I would have had no trouble believing them. After just one night under its roof the house felt like home to me, and Clarissa and Poldo, though a good ten years too young for the purpose and as unparental as they come, made convincing enough stand-ins in my imagination for the mother and father I wished I'd had.

I felt resentful, almost jealous, therefore, when I learnt that another guest of roughly my own age was to be added to our number. Things were so perfect as they were, why go and spoil them? I wasn't *that* sure we even needed William. The name: Stevie, and the protective flurry of preparations – airing of bedroom, beating of mattress, special non-pork ham ordered from Perugia, special non-fibre pillow to be bought at the chemists' – made me automatically anticipate a girl and I disliked her intensely right up to the moment when she made her appearance as a seventeen-year-old, very gauche, very shy American male. Then I felt ashamed of myself. You couldn't dislike Stevie. Be jealous of Stevie. Nobody could. Stevie was an innocent, a Candide, a babe in the holm oak wood into which he now found himself parachuted. Son of a movie mogul, reared in orthodox Jewry and privately educated on account of throttling asthma which was only now beginning to release its grip, he had never left the States before – probably not even in his imagination. And now all of a sudden here he was, jetlagged and homesick, making his first acquaintance with the inhabitants of the Old World. An illicit couple, a scarlet woman, two were-wolves, an Oscar Wilde look-alike – poor Stevie, no, for him you could only feel a tender compassion.

He slipped so neatly, too, into our layabout routine. His orthodoxy, his asthma, both of which at the outset had seemed so taxing from the housekeeping point of view, made no discernible demands on anyone, even on himself. He ate omnivorously, he slept, he swam, he slept again, and in his few waking intervals he smiled his bemused smile and agreed to everything that was said to him and/or suggested. I'm not sure whether during his entire stay he ever really knew he was awake. It could easily be that when the jet shipped him home again and he came to in his Californian ocean-view bedroom, slightly the worse for all the Cuba Libres Poldo had plied him with in lieu of Coke, it was with the feeling of having dreamed a long, senseless and totally irrelevant dream.

Maybe the night of the ballet, though, would have left a slight mark. That was quite an evening, what with the Monsignore and Ravel's Bolero and our walk along the viaduct and the rest.

It was the night before William arrived, I remember that clearly because there was the problem the next day of how much to tell him and how much not. A stuffy, thundery night promising storms, which never seemed to break. Our first taste – just a foretaste really, a starter, an antipasto – of bad Italian weather.

The Monsignore had come in the afternoon to talk to Arianna about the annulment that her wronged husband was, to newspaper readers' delight, seeking to obtain on sexy technical grounds of great complexity, and had stayed on, uninvited but quite impossible to budge. The cocktail of worldliness, wine, good food, and a chance to mutter smutty Latin words like *erectio, introductio,*

70

penetratio, ejaculatio to a beautiful woman had evidently gone to his head. Clarissa did her best with heavyweight hints like, 'Monsignore, perhaps you would like to come and sit inside and listen to the news while we all go and change for dinner,' or, 'Monsignore, I am sorry to have to hurry you over your brandy but we have tickets for the ballet this evening, and it begins . . . ' But in vain. He merely replied, *'Bene, bene, figliola,'* to everything she said and rubbed his hands together and grinned and trotted along behind.

No, wrong: when we left for Spoleto he trotted on before, and settled himself into Poldo's Land Rover instead of taking his own car, which was why we had to split into two groups. Had we been just us seven we would have piled ourselves into the vehicle any old how, and that would probably have been the end of the matter, but with the Monsignore's skirts and bulk spread over the two front passenger seats this was no longer possible. (Nor was it possible to ask him to make room for someone else, for the simple reason that nobody, not even Poldo with his built-in respect for the Roman Catholic clergy, trusted themselves any longer to speak to the man without cracking up entirely.)

Does this make the Monsignore responsible for what happened? Was the breadth of his skirts, like the length of Cleopatra's nose, the tiny-yet-oh-so-significant factor that determined the whole future course of events? No, of course not, no more than Clarissa's love of the ballet was responsible, or Ollie's desire for coffee afterwards, or any of the zillion little lead-up causes that got us where we got to, when we got to it. It was a happening waiting to happen. If not that night, another night. If not in that place, in another. Sooner or later Nico and William would have travelled again: Finland, North America, Canada, Central Europe – with their life style they'd have been bound to visit one or other of these places; and when they did, someone would have organized a trip to the mountains – a skiing excursion or something – and it would have happened.

Ah, yes, but what if it had happened *significantly* later when, say, Nico and William had had a child? According to Nico, Lady Sherwood was already marshalling her troops on that front, making pointed remarks about Delham's rooms being 'so empty without ankle biters' etc, so it's a safe bet that William wouldn't have held out against her much longer in Nico's favour, nor would Nico have been able to stall indefinitely in the face of their combined pressure. Admittedly she was still in her early twenties but she and William had been married three years already; on any conventional reckoning it was coming up kid time, breeding time, production of heir time. So. If that had happened before this other thing? If Nico had had a child already, what would she have done then? She'd have torn herself apart, that's what. She'd have felt the trap close around her, and half of her would have been in it and half out, and she'd have gnawed herself to death like other trapped wild creatures do in the attempt to get free.

So maybe, even if his skirts played only an infinitesimal part in what happened, I should thank the

Monsignore for spreading them. I hated the man – still do in fact, I hate everything he stands for: pomp, superstition, wiliness and slippery love of gain – but maybe in the end he turned out useful, preparing an escape route from family ties not only for the cuckolded Conte, Arianna's husband, but for Nico as well.

Anyway, upshot of it all: two separate cars to the ballet and two separate cars on the way back. Clarissa, Poldo, Arianna and the Monsignore leading the way in the Land Rover; Nico, me, Ollie and zonked-out Stevie following on in the gardener's tiny Bianchina van – close on their wheels because, even though he'd been to Spoleto several times before, Ollie still didn't know the way. He was the only one of us guests who had insurance cover and an international license, so it was he who drove.

The outward journey was a sheer joy ride. As we freewheeled down the oak grove, the wake of our bottled up laughter must have spread out behind us, glowing in the dusk like the tail of a comet or the sky-stripe of a jet. Another Faustian, soul-forfeiting moment, so similar to the earlier one on the return trip from Delham that looking back on it I almost discern a pattern: an Up before a Down, a High before a Hurtle. They say things always come in threes, so it occurred to me afterwards that if ever, by some crazy chance, I should find myself for a third time speeding along in a car with Nico, my spirits soaring, my stomach muscles screaming for repose, I should start seriously to prepare myself for yet another dive.

The ballet sobered us up a bit, but not for long. True, the choreographer had put a fashionable left wing social slant on the production, placing a big sort of wine press affair in the centre of his round stage and dressing his dancers as what Ollie kept loudly referring to as Revolting Peasants, but the pulse of Ravel's Bolero lends itself to other more intimate readings as well, and Ollie immediately set about giving us one. Leaning forward so as to be heard easily by the Monsignore, who was sitting between Clarissa and Arianna in the row in front, he began labelling the various stages of the crescendo with pompous Latin-sounding names akin to the ones the Monsignore himself had used that afternoon, starting, if I remember rightly, with *Collaptio, Floptio* etc, and working on through *Tittilatio, Dilatio, Inflatio, Grand Sensatio* until, with a gasp that was audible above the last shattering drum roll, he reached Agghh! *Climatio*!!!

It was silly, schoolboy humour, OK, but, wound up as we were by the context and the music, it was impossible to resist. For Arianna it may not have been so hard, she didn't have much of a sense of fun, not the verbal sort of fun anyway, but poor Clarissa – I don't know how she coped. Now and again she would turn round, puce in the face with mock fury and the effort of keeping serious, and hiss at Ollie, 'Stop it, you beast! Stop it, or else . . . !' But then laughter would get the better of her and she would have to face the stage again and simulate a coughing fit. Poldo with his Catholic upbringing was possibly a little shocked, but even he

74

kept on snorting helplessly into his hanky; while Nico, Stevie and I just clung to one another, oblivious to audience disapproval, and moaned. The fact that Stevie hadn't a clue what he was laughing at, or who the Monsignore was, or what the pseudo-Latin words meant, or why Ollie was inventing them, added a fey kind of nonsense element, and in the end it was this rather than the joke itself that amused us most.

A pretty memorable evening, even had it finished there. But it didn't, nowhere near. To shield the Monsignore from any further mickey-taking, Poldo and Clarissa hustled him away, together with Arianna, the moment the show was over, leaving us four trouble-makers to follow on whenever we felt like it. The implication being that the later we felt like it the better.

'You know the way home now, *don't* you. You'll all want to see something of Spoleto, *won't* you.' Clarissa fired at us over her shoulder. She had mastered her mirth now, or at least got it under temporary wraps, and her words were not questions, they were orders. Enough, you goofy fifth formers. Game over.

So we drifted out into the square in the flux of the departing audience and began looking for a suitable café for Ollie, who wanted an espresso, and for Stevie, who we decided *needed* an espresso, double or even triple, if we were not to end up dumping him on a bench or carrying him back to the car pick-a-back, fast asleep. But the search was not as easy as it sounded. All the cafés were open and brightly lit and welcoming, and we passed at least a dozen of them, but by 'suitable'

Ollie said he meant somewhere quiet where there was nobody he knew sitting inside needing to be greeted, and this, the festival being a festival and Ollie being Ollie, proved a hard condition to fulfil.

'Every queer that ever there was . . . ' he began singing ruefully to the tune of the Teddy Bears' Picnic, and led us higher and higher up the stone-paved streets of the town until at last, in the lee of the great Albornoz fortress that bestrides its summit, we reached a zone that was poorly lit, almost in darkness, and here he sat down on a wall to get his breath back.

'Hey-ho. One more chance. If I remember rightly there ought to be a hotel just round that bend at the end there. But if not, then that's it. No coffee, no nothing. Spoleto stops here. Literally, and rather *over*-dramatically for my taste.' He tutted crossly. 'A little Umbrian town behaving as if it were in the Alps. Such cheek. Although mind you, with all this climbing . . . '

The hotel was there, all right, and its bar was just as open and inviting as the other places, if not more so, but it didn't meet with Ollie's prime requirement either. 'Oh my god, no!' he exclaimed after a cautious peer into the lobby, 'Dragomir, the greasy Pole!'

So that was that. Lid on the coffee pot. Seeing that we had come this far, however, Ollie now suggested, in an oddly Baedekery mood for him, that we ought perhaps to take a look at the famous viaduct that linked Spoleto to the neighbouring mountain of Monteluco. He didn't think much of these great brooding constructions himself, mind you, he was careful to add, and it was too dark for proper sightseeing, but still, this one was fairly spectacular – *if* your taste ran to medieval meccano – and it couldn't be more than a hundred yards distant, if that.

A hundred yards. The length of a football pitch, and the plan, design, random cosmic doodle or whatever, was complete. In fact it would have been slightly under a hundred yards, because I remember that the curve of the first massive arch had begun to loom at us out of the darkness, but we had not yet set foot on the walled walkway of the viaduct proper, when it happened.

Happened? Well, nothing happened really, nothing special, nothing you'd even notice unless your attention was called back to it later. We were wandering along in single file, straggling a bit by then: Ollie in front, me following, and the other two a short distance behind, when suddenly I felt a brushing movement against my bare leg, and saw Ollie stagger slightly sideways as if he had tripped up or stubbed his foot against a stone.

'Oy!' He said. 'What was that?' And I said automatically, 'What was what?' Not paying much attention at all. And then Ollie made a kind of puffing, Oh forget it, noise, and we plodded on, and it wasn't until we were half way across the viaduct, where there is a small arch-shaped opening set into the wall like a window, and we were peering down through it into the inky blackness of the ravine below, that Stevie suddenly said, 'Hey, but where's Nico? Where's the Duchess?' And I realised – lamentably late – that Nico was missing.

7

My hearing range is as wide as Nico's – why was it, then, that I didn't pick up the same message that she did and react to it in the same way? I don't know, I still can't explain it, not completely. Probably the French-man in the train was right: these things take time, and I just wasn't ready.

That it reached me at some level of consciousness is almost certain, though, because when Stevie announced his discovery I wasn't worried at all. I was surprised, yes; hurt by the haste and stealth with which Nico had scarpered, yes; I felt excluded, slighted, miffed, all sorts of niggling things, but I wasn't worried. Only, that is, about how to explain to the others her disappearance in convincing terms that wouldn't discredit her entirely. I knew she'd turn up sooner or later – probably later; and I knew what she'd look like when she did: i.e. a total mess, as if she'd been living it up with the raggle taggle gypsies-o. Which was not so far from the truth, because she had switched, that's what she'd done. Reverted. It was clear as Perspex. She'd sensed the presence of something strongly alluring in the forest on the far side of the ravine – what would it have been? What *could* it have been? A deer? A badger? A wild boar? Most likely a wild boar: Poldo said the woods were teeming with them – and without so much as a 'Sorry, Sarah, I'm off', still less a 'Want to come with me?' she had darted past me, nearly flooring Ollie in the process, and forsaken me. Forsaken *me*, her faithful familiar who would accompany her to Hell and back (and had been part of the way there with her already, remember), for a glorified bristle-covered pig that would probably chuck her out of its territory with one flick of its tusks, and serve her right.

If this last had been the case, however, she would have come back earlier. I had plenty of time to mull over this unwelcome truth and its riders as the night progressed, or rather as it dragged on into early morning, and as Ollie and Stevie and I dragged ourselves around in it, calling out Nico's name and bickering among ourselves as to what to do, and still no sign of her return. Stevie was all for packing in our search and going to the police. He was convinced something dramatic had happened to Nico like a kidnapping, or a fall, or a memory loss, or even a permutation of the three, and kept gabbling on about this Canadian friend of his who had hit his head in a skiing accident and had forgotten everything (except, presumably, his ski technique) and had gone on whirling round the pistes like a crazed hamster on a tread-wheel until the lifts had closed down and he'd been brought to a stop.

Ollie in contrast was dead against the police idea: he didn't say so but I think he thought Nico was on drugs and had simply met up with a pusher and was taking time out for a fix. Instead he was in favour of ringing Clarissa to tell her what was happening and maybe get her to ask Poldo to telephone the hospital to check on admissions, just in case.

I, naturally, was against doing anything. Except hang around in the vicinity of the car park and wait for Nico to come back. Hopefully not looking too rough. Although rough or smooth, her reputation was going to suffer for this folly anyway: Ollie would see to that once he got back to London again, and into his professional stride. I warned Nico about this the next morning, hoping it would sting her vanity and have some effect. 'Go on like this and people will start shunning you,' I said. 'They'll cut you out of the social swim. Is that what you want to happen? Is that really what you want?' Daft question and dafter phrasing. Nico hardly bothered to reply, just tossed her head, flipping the question carelessly over in her mind pancake-fashion, and then with an, 'Oh, no, I'm all for social swims, think I'll have one now,' plunged into the pool. From that morning on she did a lot of swimming, now I come to think of it. Churning up and down, length after length, and slapping into the borders on each turn as if she resented them being there.

But anyway, that night, by means of keeping Ollie and Stevie continually on the move, shunting them from bar to bar and café to café and then back to the car again for just one more check, I somehow managed to prevent either of them from putting his scheme into action. I harried them, chivvied them, didn't give them time to do anything practical at all. Until finally – it must have been nearly dawn by then – on about our seventh or eighth trip to the car park, there Nico stood, leaning against the bonnet of the car, grinding a cigarette butt into the ground with her shoe, as if nothing particular were the matter and if anything we, and not she, were the ones who were late.

I could have clobbered her, I was so relieved. So underneath my cloak of calm I must have been worrying all along unawares: the night forest is not a safe place to hang out in, and that goes for all creatures, great, middling and small. The three of us rushed towards her, firing questions, and I saw her step fastidiously back. Even if not aimed at me particularly, the gesture stung. She was looking oddly composed for someone who'd been on a wild boar hunt. And also, in some way I couldn't quite put my finger on straight off, different. Smaller, that was it, she looked smaller. And some of her radiance had gone: under the harsh neon lighting of the parking lot her hair was tow coloured and her eyes looked spent, almost sad.

'What do you mean, where was I?' She asked, yawning cigarette smoke into our faces. 'Where were *you*, all of you? I've been looking everywhere.' This was said flatly – take it or leave it. She clearly couldn't be bothered with us – any of us. She couldn't even be bothered to concoct a decent lie.

She couldn't be bothered to tell me much about her jaunt, either, when I questioned her on our way to bed. Or at least so I interpreted her brief, throwaway

81

description at the time. 'Didn't amount to much,' she shrugged. 'There's not a lot goes on in these woods. Shooters have blasted them dry. Empty cartridge cases all over the place. Boars? Yeah, probably quite a few, judging by the spoors, but they keep to their dens or wherever and I don't blame them. Heard an owl once or twice. For the rest it was mostly moths.'

Moths? Nothing else but moths? I couldn't believe this. 'No mice or things? No porcupines?' I remembered quite clearly Poldo saying there were porcupines as well as boars.

'Saw a dead one of those,' she admitted after a slight hesitation. 'Snared. Oh, yes, and saw a family of foxes. Scruffy old vixen with her dugs flapping, litter of cubs playing around in the carcass of a rusty old fridge. It's that sort of scene. Pathetic really. You didn't miss anything, relax. Mind if we don't talk about it anymore?'

Mind? I did mind, of course I did, I minded desperately. I minded anything that set distance between us, or even threatened to do so, but I was wise enough to keep this fact to myself. Offence, umbrage, chippiness, reproach – one drop of any of these in the brew of a friendship, and that friendship is as good as poisoned. Who taught me this? No one, just a merciful instinct.

The rest of the holiday went by with no further mishaps. But no further enchantment either. In my memory the first part is sunlit, and the second part, following our trip to Spoleto and William's subsequent arrival, lies in faint but discernible shadow. Nothing gloomy, merely as if a few wispy clouds had placed themselves between us and the sun. I don't recall William's nose getting burnt either, which he complained it always did in the summertime, pretty dramatically, even in England, so it may be that the clouds were for real.

They were certainly real enough over the Channel when we flew back. I was still smarting inside from what I considered Nico's treachery, and what with that and the grey sky and the post-holiday feel, I was not greatly looking forward to picking up the tatty threads of our recent London life. To make matters worse, since her night out in Spoleto Nico's restlessness had come back in force – it happens with hawks too, I read somewhere: a night in the open and a bird will never again submit to training – and I could therefore see more vodka on the horizon, and more scuffed shoes and mangled clothes and headaches and hangovers, to the point where I began wondering whether I could stand the pace. Did I really love Nico enough to pickle my liver and ruin my entire wardrobe for her sake?

I think I probably did, considering what I am preparing to do now, but I was never put to that particular test. Because this time Nico's fidgets led us off on quite a different tack. I hadn't noticed any particular signs of her metamorphosis on the plane, or even on our first evening back at Sherwood House, only that she was very quiet and thoughtful for her and made no telephone calls where I had been expecting dozens, but the morning after, the process was complete and there she was in a brand new form. Fresh from the chrysalis. Or, no, other way round, fresh into the chrysalis, because from jaded social butterfly in search of thrills she had turned into an apprentice bookworm, as eager to acquire knowledge as her forerunner had been to blot it out. Probably a false memory, because her eyesight was good for a semi-canine, but I even seem to remember her wearing a pair of tortoiseshell specs to lend her face an extra touch of seriousness. And – nothing false about this one, thank god – her eyes, whether shielded by lenses or not, had that tiny, jewel-like lick of flame in them again: different maybe, more questioning, less debonair, but somewhere behind them still lurked the Nico of old.

'Oh, Sarie. Best and only. I woke up this morning and I suddenly realised: I'm useless. What have I done with my life so far? Nothing. I'm just taking up space. I'm no good to anyone. I know nothing. My education is abysmal. Say someone were to ask me, What's the moon made of? Or, Where does electricity come from? Or, How do you set a broken leg? I wouldn't have a clue what to say. It's shaming.'

'What about those O levels you got at school?' She'd told me once she had passed in eight subjects; I'd been quite impressed. 'You'd never have got all those unless you'd learned *something*.'

'Oh, piff,' she said. 'O levels. I learnt how to lift things off the page for a while and store them in my head till I wrote them down on an exam paper, that's all. But once I'd written them they were gone. Nothing stayed, nothing really made any mark on my brain at all. And yet . . . '

Little note of anxiousness creeping in. ' . . . I've got one, haven't I, Sarie? Wouldn't you say I've got a brain? Good enough to . . . I don't know, to go to university, for example? I mean . . . William went to Oxford . . . '

I'd never given much thought to Nico's brain, or mine either for that matter, but put like that she had a point. She was definitely cleverer than William, we both were. Worse educated but far quicker on the uptake. 'Why?' I said, feeling a sudden little stirring of excitement: perhaps, with Nico to spur me on, I too could aspire to something a bit more challenging than a secretarial course. 'You weren't thinking of going to university *now*, were you? No, because . . . '

She cut me short. 'I was,' she said. 'I am. Why not? Why don't we put ourselves down for some university somewhere and really start studying? Something important we can get our teeth into?'

Our teeth. That was part of the problem. But there were others too. 'Because I think you have to have at least three A levels to get into any university, even the crummiest,' I finished. 'And we've got none, so we're stumped.'

'No, we're not. Don't be so defeatist. We'll get them, silly. We'll go back to sodding school if need be and sodding well get them. I could do English, French and Italian, and you could do English, French and . . . What was your best subject at school? Maths? Seriously? No joking? Then you could do Maths. Won't take us long, not if we really work at it. Few months, that's all.'

Put like that it sounded easy, but then came the

hurdles. Chief and rather unexpected of which was William himself.

'It's a godawful horrendous idea,' he cried out in dismay when Nico put it to him. 'Think if the papers get wind of it. Think what fun they'll have: Society Belle, or whatever it is they call you, Goes Back to School. Think if you fail, too. They'll do a piece on you like they did on the guests at Pug's wedding, only it'll be the upper class forehead, their target, instead of the upper class chin.'

Nico brushed this objection scornfully aside. 'Oh for God's sake, Will, sometimes you can be so *stuffy*. What's newsworthy about studying? Nothing. Journalists only come after you if you have an affair with a footballer or go to Ascot with a hernia truss on your head. You know that perfectly well. No one's going to give a shit about my A levels or whether I pass them or fail.'

'Aren't they just? I think you underestimate your press appeal, my lovely.'

'I think you *over*rate it,' she snapped back. 'And it's no good looking at Sarah like that. It's not her plan, it's mine. *I* want to learn. *I* want to study.'

'I'm sure it's yours,' he said, a shade bitterly for him. 'But study what, for Christ's sake?'

At this Nico floundered slightly. 'I don't know, I haven't really thought yet. Anything. Something. Something useful, something that tells you about the way the world's made, something . . . ' She found a word but you could see she knew it wasn't the right one even before she uttered it, 'scientific.'

86

William was quick to pounce on it. 'Something scientific! Honestly, Nico, I thought you'd do better than that. What scientific? Scientific what? Chemistry? Molecular biology? Genetics? Physics? Electronic engineering? What? Where did you get this sudden learning lust from when you don't even know what discipline interests you?'

Nico's cheekbones flushed abruptly as if an invisible passerby had spotted them with rouge. 'That's just it, don't you see? I don't know. Can't you see my point? I hardly even know what all these things are. Why they're different, how they're different. If I knew, I wouldn't be so ignorant; and if I wasn't so ignorant I wouldn't be so desperately in need of tuition, would I?'

'OK, OK, no need to get het up about it.' William was unable to deal with any show of female emotion, even if it was just two small red spots of warning on a cheek. 'But why exams, why university? Why not just read books on the subject? Once you get round to picking a subject, that is.'

'Because. Because. Oh, can't you see, Will? I want to do something useful with my life. Useful to others. You ought to approve, surely. Must be better than boozing, no? Must be better than just traipsing around to parties and getting sloshed.'

'And those are your only alternatives?'

It was funny. It had just struck me: when Nico had said, 'It's no good looking at Sarah like that,' William hadn't been looking at me at all. He'd been looking at her. In fact he and she had been looking at each other steadfastly during this entire exchange, and were still doing so, with a pathos that had nothing to do with their surface behaviour. There was a subtext running under their spoken words, that was it. William had his fair share of aristocratic aplomb – far milder than his mum's but it was there: he wasn't *really* worried about what the press might say. The opinion of anyone who had to learn things about him or his wife from a newspaper was by that very token immaterial to him. No, with his questions he was in effect asking Nico, 'What's wrong? Why can't you be happy with me when I do everything I can to make you so? Why can't you settle down, be a proper wife, have children?' And she was replying, 'I don't know, that's the tragedy of it, but have patience with me, I beg. Don't press me. Let me find my own way.'

Which in the end was what William did, of course. He had no choice. But he caved in gracefully none the less. He even gave us the address of a crammer in North London, with whose teaching methods he seemed to be suspiciously familiar. Nico and I, when we went there, took one look at the outside of the building and fled. Nico could act unglamorously but only up to a certain point: to attend such an establishment in the company of the pupils we saw mooching through its entrance, scattering behind them trails of dandruff and dejection, was beyond it. Instead we procured copies of the relevant syllabuses, booked ourselves into the summer GCE session of a local grammar school (where William's aunt was on the board of governors, but never mind about that), and set about cramming ourselves.

8

And so began our study period. Nico and my school-days together. A term, roughly speaking: close on four calendar months. But in my memory these months spread out like a conjuror's magic hanky to enwrap a whole chunk of my life – an age, almost an era.

Because mental toil binds too, I was forgetting that. Memorizing is a solitary business, but memorizing isn't everything in the learning process, it's only the final act of storage. The other phases that precede it – the reading, the research, the grasping, the making connections – all these can be done working in tandem. No physical mingling of liquids, OK, but a trickling of ideas into a shared channel; most of them worthless and fit only for flushing, but one or two better ones flowing along together, picking up speed and substance as they go.

I deliberately don't say clarity. I have never thought so hard, read so hard, argued so hard as Nico and I did during that time: you'd have thought instead of four subjects for a school level exam we were swotting for an all round knowledge quiz to win us a fortune. But of clarity, not a trace. Nico was almost impossible to keep on track. Like the borders of the swimming pool, the confines of the syllabus didn't guide her, they just seemed to get in her way. It was no good, for example, pointing out to her that we had to concentrate on *Twelfth Night* for our English Literature paper: she wanted First Night though to Thirty Eighth or what-ever the total of Shakespeare's plays amounts to – the whole collection.

And the same with a vengeance applied to the actual range of subjects we had chosen. Astronomy, music, natural history, geography, medicine – none of these things figured on our minimal fourfold list, but that fact didn't seem to deter her in the slightest from wanting to explore them. In a way it was frustrating: I had to keep lassoing her, roping her in, reminding her like a prim school goody-goody of the goal we were trying to achieve. But in another way it was exhilarating. Every single day practically she came up with a new topic of investigation. Music in particular obsessed her – or, better, her ignorance of it did. 'What are these Gold-berg whatsits everyone makes such a fuss of? Put them on our shopping list, Sarah, write them down. We've got to hear them, can't afford not to. Both the Passions too. Much of Bach as we can gobble. Schubert and Chopin, same thing: oughtn't say so but in a way it's lucky they died young or we'd never even get halfway. Oh oh, hold it. Says on the sleeve here Verdi's Falstaff is a must. Verdi died old, trust him. Never heard of it, never knew it existed. Put that down too.'

It's a wonder she didn't make me play all these discs at seventy-eight revs in order to get through more stuff.

In one of my maths books there was a paragraph on a certain mathematician – Evariste Galois he was called, or maybe it was Gallois with two l's – who, aged twenty, as he set out for the duel that was to kill him, had scribbled on the margin of the proof he had just completed, 'So little time, so little time.' Well, that was Nico for you. She shovelled knowledge into herself like a squirrel on the brink of winter shovels nuts. Quick, quick, lay in a store, the frost is coming. The bill from Hatchards, which was the only book fount she and I knew how to tap, must have been enormous. The one from the record store likewise. However, apart from teetering slightly on his chair at breakfast when he opened their brown invoice envelopes, William never gave the slightest sign of disapproval or uttered a word of reproof.

Poor William, poor kind patient William, he was more disoriented than I was by the course events were taking. I at least, scurrying along behind her, could keep in some kind of mental contact with Nico. Or so I fancied. In fact there were times – not many, but there were times – when I had never felt so close. I can remember us, for example, one late afternoon, lying noses in the air on the rug in front of the fire listening to a Schubert piano sonata – I've forgotten which one, but it has an opening of a single note from which the rest of the sonata blossoms out gently like a flower from a seed: one note, two notes, eight notes, thirteen and away – and I remember on the second eight-note sequence Nico and I turning to face one another, and my seeing through the panes of her eyes everything that was going on inside my own head: the same deep swirl of loosely formed thoughts about life and the cosmos and what we were doing in it and whether there was any point or logic to anything, and then the same little puddle of calm suddenly forming in the middle of the swirl and spreading outwards in step with the music: one, two, eight, thirteen and so on until all was flat and peaceful as a pond. She said something, something like, 'All these theories, all these puzzles, and it's all so simple really.' But I didn't even need this pointer. Our minds were in total communion: it was as if we had no scalps, no skulls, nothing in the way to stop the thoughts merging. Siamese twins sharing a brain. It could have been eerie: in fact it felt totally natural, and eerie was the feeling when the walls went up again and each of us retreated into her own bounded space.

Such moments of nearness made the separation, when it came, all the more difficult to understand and accept. (More difficult? Blockhead! What *am* I saying? If a thing is already impossible it can't become more difficult. And this thing was truly impossible: you might as well ask a guillotined head to understand and accept the falling of the blade.) On December 23rd Nico and William went to Italy again to stay with Clarissa. A neighbouring house was up for sale and she and Poldo wanted them to have a look at it with a view to buying. Nico, who may have relished the secret irony of the term, had often of late expressed her wish for an

Italian 'bolthole'. I was to spend Christmas with my parents and then fly out and join the four of them for New Year.

Mundane arrangements, all very straightforward and simple. I left Sherwood House the night before Nico and William did – their plane was due to depart early the next morning – so there was no drama to our parting and I paid it scant attention. Was Nico in a particularly odd mood? Did she do or say anything that should have alerted me? Nothing that stuck in my mind, so presumably not. Recently she had mentioned something about a friend – another Clarissa as chance would have it – who had committed suicide the year before, but it was only a passing mention. And it was nothing very memorable anyway. 'Wonder if took guts? Wonder how she felt before she did it?' A casual remark like that; it made no impression until later, when I cast around so desperately in my head for signs.

She was upstairs, packing, when we said goodbye. Strewing clothes all over the place and rattling on as she did so about this little kid – the son of some much travelled friend or other – who always asked before leaving for Italy whether it was Hot Italy they were taking him to or Cold Italy, convinced they were two distinct countries. 'And this'll be Cold Italy,' I remember her adding, 'This'll be Fucking Freezing Italy.'

But I don't remember seeing her pack many warm clothes. Or her study books either. She had a ragged old sheepskin jacket someone had brought her from Mongolia which she wore everywhere with great panache, even to balls. She called it mockingly her 'fur' and kept it stuffed into a recess of the outside portico, complaining that the central heating made it smell. I reminded her not to forget it because she might need it.

She smiled and repeated my words to herself in a singsong tone I found almost childish at the time, and that now seems to me so poignant it hardly bears contemplating. 'I may be needing my fur. I may be needing my fur.'

9

It was Freezing Italy all right when I reached it, summoned by a garbled telegram sent off from the local post office by one of Clarissa's otherwise perfect domestics. The text of the message was so eccentric that the operator who relayed it to me over the telephone could hardly contain her laughter. For a fraction of a second it sounded funny to me too, but only for a fraction, before the knell sounded. Nico involved mortal incident stop come kick Gugliam. It was the word mortal that did it. Mortal is mortal, it admits no fudging; it sheds gravitas like a pall over every sentence that contains it.

But I still didn't connect it to Nico. I kept the two words forcibly apart in my head until I had rung the villa. I got Poldo on the line, who passed me over to Clarissa without a word. From the way I heard him whisper my name to her I already feared the worst, and yet when my fears were confirmed I found myself asking, begging, imploring that it not be so. 'True?' She said. 'Oh yes, I'm so sorry, Sarah, it's true all right. That ghastly aqueduct – she leaped off it into the void. No doubts at all: a man saw her go; he said she climbed onto the window ledge and dived off headfirst before

95

he could stop her. We should have sent the telegram ourselves, I know, only we've been so plagued. The police and things – you can't imagine the horror of it all. Suicide in Italy is looked on practically as a crime. William? No, he's out. Like a boxer, I mean: we've drugged him. But he wants you to come immediately, I know he does. He said to get in touch with Ollie and have him accompany you. Oh yes, and to get the ticket money off Stewart if you're short.'

William, Clarissa, Poldo, Ollie. Collalto, the villa, the holm oaks, the dogs. Everything the same and yet everything so different. A dank fog where there had been sunlight. Macks in the hall where we had hung our bathing towels. Frost-shrivelled plants in the borders; the fruit trees bare and dripping; the pool covered by a dark green tarpaulin sheet on which floated leaves trapped in ice, and the fanned out wing feathers of a dead bird. Fucking Freezing Italy, and in it somewhere, not that distant, Nico's body, cold as well.

The house was busy when Ollie and I entered; the phone was ringing, voices were coming from the drawing room, and members of the hitherto invisible staff were flitting all over the place, but the busyness was cheerless. Italians react angrily to the death of a young person, I discovered: you could sense this anger in the atmosphere. Anger and pain, and I brought a whole lot more of both with me.

I so shrank from meeting William I felt almost ill. In fact I was ill, I had developed some kind of flu bug on the plane, but my throat ached so hard of its own accord and my eyes and nose streamed so constantly from crying that I barely noticed.

What I did notice though, and almost immediately, was that I was now an outsider. My link to this world, to these people, had passed exclusively through Nico. With her death, it was severed. Oh, they were kind to me all right. Clarissa rushed over and hugged me, Poldo too; Nico's mother, just in from Brazil, clasped me fleetingly to her vicuña-clad breast; even the truculent Dowager Marchioness was gracious enough to plant a kiss in the air in the vicinity of my ear lobe and remember my name without being prompted. 'So tragic, Sarah dear, so tragic. So young, so beautiful . . . Such a bitter blow for William.' But I was no longer one of them.

Only to William was there still some kind of living connection, but I could tell that it embarrassed him, so after our initial gaping into one another's eyes in agony at our loss, I kept my distance.

I wasn't allowed to visit the body. Something to do with police regulations. Perhaps it was better that way. My wanting to was for some reason considered by everyone, William included, rather tasteless.

So I withdrew into myself still further. Ollie hovered round me, filling the role of *cavalier servente* as bidden, but his performance was less convincing than it had been on the plane: he could see my star had already waned. I didn't hold this against him – a court jester occupies a delicate position halfway between confidant and menial – Ollie had his balancing work cut out.

At the funeral, which took place in Spoleto next morning, early and in great secret in order to dodge the journalists, he and I sat together in the rear of the church, separated from the other mourners by several rows of empty pews. My mind retains little of the scene: probably I was still half anesthetised by shock. I recall the intense cold and a jumble of words – in which language, Latin or Italian, I couldn't make out, but it was a catholic rite. Strange when the Sherwoods were protestant, but it was probably all that was on offer. William was past caring about such things anyway; Nico's mum I think was a catholic convert herself due to one of her marriages; and Lady Sherwood clearly didn't give a fig what liturgy the service came from as long as it was over quickly. I also remember the big red cross of roses sliding off the coffin as it was brought in. That, and a bat hanging from one of the rafters, and Ollie rolling up bits of his hymn card or mass card or whatever into little balls and flicking them at it in an attempt to get it to fly. I figure he was bored and relished the idea of a bit of a diversion.

I wasn't bored though. I wasn't sad either because sad implies you have something left to feel with. I wasn't anything, I was empty – cold and dark and empty, like the Nico-less life that spread itself out before me. She was gone so completely that no part of this charade had anything to do with her. Or with me either. It had been a mistake to come.

Halfway through the ceremony I left Ollie to his flicking and got up and walked out of the church.

Having gone through the summer dress rehearsal with such thoroughness and done such diligent to-ing and fro-ing through the town, my feet knew exactly what path to take. Up they carried me, up and up the narrow stony street, past the cafés – most of them closed at this time of year – under the bastions of the fortress, past the spot where Ollie had rested, round the last bend and in front of the hotel, until I came in sight of the great aqueduct with its lopsided-walled bridge leading across the rift valley between the two mountains. And there, set into the centre of the higher wall, drawing the eye towards it as irresistibly as a plughole draws water, was the small semicircular aperture through which Nico had jumped. Her Italian bolthole.

The scene of two desertions on her part, two betrayals, and this one so final it was as if on exiting she had slammed that window right in my face and then barred it to make double sure I stayed put. I could forgive her for leaving the world on her own terms – everyone has a right to do that: death right is our birthright – but I couldn't forgive her for not telling me she was going, or at the very least leaving me a message. And yet forgive I must, or the bitterness would cause my heart to harden against her, and it would end up cured and indifferent, and dry as a hunk of stockfish. (Is that why they say 'cured' of hams and things, I wonder? Dried amounting to cured?) In a way that would be the worst result of all: I would lose her entirely, even the memories.

Already I could feel them subtly changing in my

mind. Our winter afternoons of study, with our fags and our cups of hot chocolate and our books spread out on the table under the library window – those sessions had been so happy at the time that . . . We'd been so happy at the time that . . . See what I mean? Wrong, all wrong. *I'd* been so happy at the time. Nico would have been anything but: she would have been confused, depressed getting on fast towards acutely miserable. And she'd never let on, never given a sign. The whole idea of studying and entering university, although possibly genuine to begin with, must have gone dead on her at some point and she'd just carried on out of habit, inertia, or else with the deliberate aim of concealing from William and me her real intentions. You don't jump off a bridge and into a rocky crevasse hundreds of feet below on a whim of the moment. An action like that has a colossal build-up of anguish behind it.

So, Nico was in anguish and I never even noticed. How close did that set me in her affections? Light years away. Dark impenetrable light years away. Those recent visits to the dentist where she never wanted me to accompany her. 'No, Sarie, you stay in and mug up about that tiresome Wife of Bath – the raunchy old cow. Do it for both of us, right? I don't want to you to see me at Mr Penny's mercy. Besides, I shan't be able to keep a straight face if you're there: coming up lunch-time his tummy always rumbles like an earthquake.' Pantomime. Nico's teeth were perfect; there'd been nothing wrong with them ever. She'd never been near the dentist's. Where had she been to instead? Anywhere, I should imagine. Out. Walkabout. Away. And why? In order to be alone. In order to escape from me and William – the two people in theory close enough to notice what was going on inside her. Her unquenchable thirst for knowledge? Sham, all sham. Dust thrown in our eyes to blind us to her real purpose: namely to come back here at the first opportunity and finish off what she had left undone.

Because this was the key point. Something had happened here, on this very bridge, that summer night when she had made her first solo sortie, her first escape. To borrow William's expression (a platitude but he seemed to draw comfort from it: after all, it's a plain fact of nature that if a person loses their balance they fall), something had happened to disturb the balance of her mind and from then on she had known no peace.

But *what* had happened exactly? What epiphany had Nico seen? Or heard, or smelt, or just plain sensed? Slowly I walked along the footpath, straining my senses every inch of the way. A blend of Geiger counter, scout and sniffing bloodhound: anyone watching me would have thought I was deranged.

When I reached the half-moon opening I stopped and leaned out, trying to put myself in Nico's shoes. No, not in her shoes, she had taken them off before jumping. Together with practically everything else she'd been wearing at the time, or so Clarissa told me, part fascinated, part aghast: she had peeled off her stockings, her watch, her jewellery, removed from her body pretty well everything removable, wedding ring and underclothes included, stuffed them in her handbag and then cast that aside too. Travelling light. The only thing she had taken with her into the void, apart from a loose kind of shift affair as covering, was a copy of Blake's *Songs of Innocence and Experience*, which had been found still in her hand, clasped tight. Not a syllabus book, nor one I remember her particularly liking, but evidently one she had been reading and thinking about right up to the very end. What did that mean? Nothing, it meant nothing, it merely confirmed the bleakness of her mood. William had shown me the volume: the last four lines of the closing poem were underlined in eye pencil, and Nico had drawn a kind of frame around them as well. Like the border on a mourning card:

> 'The human dress is forged iron,
> The human form a fiery forge,
> The human face a furnace sealed,
> The human heart its hungry gorge.'

It doesn't get much grimmer than that. What can it have felt like to touch such a low ebb? To be so nauseated with the world that anything seems preferable to remaining on its surface, even hurling yourself off an eighty metre high bridge and smashing yourself to pulp?

I leant over the parapet as far as I dared – which wasn't very far: I get vertigo on a stepladder. I was sad too, I was low too, but the thought of jumping made me recoil in horror. I couldn't even keep it in my mind for a second. Which meant I couldn't understand anyone who had done. Which meant I couldn't understand Nico. Which meant I had lost her in my body, and lost her in my head, and that sooner or later, no matter how hard I tried not to, I would lose her in my heart too – in my shrivelled slab-of-stockfish heart.

I hated this place with all the hatred I could summon. The hatred was a physical sensation that burned in my throat. I'd hated it already the first time round when the air was warm and soft and Nico was alive and my strongest emotion was a mild stab of pique; imagine now, in the harsh cold of winter, with Nico dead and about to be placed in a box under the ground, and my grief so raw I couldn't bear to touch it. That it happened to be one of the most beautiful spots I had ever seen, merely went to fuel the hatred.

Time to leave it before it etched itself indelibly on my memory. Which in outline it already had done, of course, twice over, in its summer night version and its winter day. The steep wooded flanks of the ravine spanned by those huge grey brick parabolas; the narrow ribbon of path leading across their top; the little semicircular hole half way along, and the terrible plunging vortex of the well shaft below – asleep or awake, I would never again be totally free of these shapes; they would lie in wait for me, coiled up in

103

everyday objects, and then spring out of them to haunt me. A 'V' on an ad hoarding, a pair of converging lines, a half moon, a segment of orange, or even maybe a croquet hoop, and back here I would be, plonked, protesting, right down in the middle of this detested spot. But still, no point in lingering and picking up more detail.

I drew back from the window and was about to turn and retrace my steps when I saw it. The visitation. The sight that Nico must have seen. The thing that, with its rare combination of drabness and magnificence, of strangeness and familiarity, must unwittingly have lured her to her death. It was a wolf. Youngish I would say. Shy too, wary, diffident, probably only goaded into the open like this by hunger. Or else attracted by some signal that my presence had sent out without my knowledge. It was standing, head raised, alert, looking straight at me, at the far end of the bridge. I'd forgotten Italy had wolves, or perhaps I'd never really thought about it. Of course, how stupid of me: Hot Italy and Cold Italy, they both had wolves.

My heart started to pump violently, partly in fear but mostly due to some other emotion I couldn't name. Zoos had been off limits to me from a very early age, so to date the only wolves I remembered seeing had been in books or films. In this two dimensional form they already affected me so deeply that I would refuse to look at any image that showed them dead or wounded: it hurt too much, came too close to the quick. But the genuine living creature – it is hard to find words for what it did to me, it held me spellbound. A milky sun had come out by then and its rays shone on the animal's head, making the little frosty beads of moisture on its fur and whiskers shine like a diadem or a frame of pearls. On a furrier's scale I suppose its coat was not that luscious, but with its variety of length and subtlety of colour – the creams, the fawns, the greys, the russets, the slates, the deep blue blacks, all worked together into one rich, tawny mélange – I wouldn't have traded it for sable. Fur, beloved texture – yes, you could say that again. I longed to get within touching distance and brush with my fingertips the thick, short, soft plush of the ears, and run my hands through the ruff of the throat, and bury my face in the deep wavy pile of the hackles. Again, probably a subjective taste that others would disagree with, but I imagined that the smell it gave off would be delicious: hot and clean and earthy, but only very faintly so. Like the paws of puppies between the pads.

But it was the eyes that fascinated me most. You can't look into human eyes like that: the brain behind resents your probing. People have things to hide; a wolf has nothing; nothing, that is, of which it need be ashamed.

Shame again. The red inkpot. Nico was right to scold me about it the way she did. Shame is human clutter, a human load, and people try to foist it on you from the moment you are born. Here, carry that, you little blighter! Too bad if your shoulders are small, you'll get used to the weight in time, everyone does.

105

The animal facing me was blessedly free of any such burden. It regarded me with total candour. Maybe it wasn't all that crazy about what it saw, maybe it even had vague plans of attack in mind, but if and when those thoughts consolidated I knew I would be able to read them in its gaze the way at present I could read simple pondering and curiosity. Like the amber whose colour they shared, the eyes were translucent. What they would look like when they showed love, loyalty, happiness, amusement and other nice things like that, I only wished I knew.

In a flash of understanding I could suddenly see why Nico had killed herself. She was a throwback like me, a genetic mishap, out of place in human society despite the position she'd achieved there, and the pull towards the clean, uncomplicated world of her wolf forbearers, once she had truly felt it, had proved too strong for her. It had been that: the yearning for a lost state of innocence – call it Arcadia if you will, or the Garden of Eden on the sixth day, early – that had rocked the balance of her mind. If I stayed here any longer or came any closer to this envoy from that earlier, simpler world I might begin to feel it myself.

Songs of Innocence and Experience. Now I could guess the wherefore of Nico's last read.

10

Perhaps I had lingered too long on the viaduct already. That night the villa that had formerly seemed home to me felt like a prison. I couldn't wait to leave the place, even though there was no other place I wanted to be instead, but there wasn't a flight until late the next day. And anyway, on our way back from the funeral William had told me, or rather whispered furtively into my ear, that there was a matter he wanted to discuss with me, and he hadn't got around to doing so yet. I wasn't that curious about what he might have to say – curiosity was another thing that had gone out of my life with Nico – but I felt I owed it to him to be patient and let him choose his time: most likely it would be after dinner when he was in his Dutch courage stage, and hopefully before he reached the Double Dutch.

Actually I did him an injustice here. It was in the drink-free gap of late afternoon that he came and sought me out. I was just in from a walk with the dogs – poor creatures, in the upheaval no one had had much time to dedicate to them – and I was sitting on a bench in the hall struggling to remove Clarissa's size five wellies from my size seven feet, when I suddenly looked up and saw him there, kneeling in front of me like a communicant or suitor, and every bit as uncomfortable.

'Need any help?'

With the boots, was what he meant, but in the larger context of our shared misery it only went to increase our awkwardness. He dreaded having to speak to me like this, on what was evidently an intimate matter: as he drew himself upright again I could literally feel the dread coming off him in waves. And I could measure it too because it exactly matched my own at having to listen. He was the mirror in which my sorrow was reflected, and vice versa I was the same to him, and neither of us wanted to be confronted by that image in the glass.

I shook my head, lowering it at the same time so that all I need see of him were his feet. They were executing a penguin-like shuffle. That odd side-to-side wriggling movement the adult bird performs as it prepares to hatch the egg.

'There was . . . Yup, there was something I wanted to say to you, Sarah. It's about . . . erm . . . well, it's about . . . '

Indistinct mumble dissolving into a series of loud swallowing noises, and then stop. He had funked it already before he'd even begun. What *would* Nico say if she could see us fiddling around in this ungainly fashion, and all because we missed her? Something pretty scathing: she would find us ludicrous, pain and all. 'For God's sake, Sarah,' I could fancy hearing her say in the ensuing silence, 'help him out of it before I clock the pair of you.'

'If it's about my leaving Sherwood House,' I tried, 'then don't worry. I'll move my stuff out as soon as I get back. I've already asked Stewart to look out for some boxes . . . '

Gasp. 'God, no. No, no, no. No, it's nothing like that. It's . . . it's . . . ' Another stall and then a sudden rush of words. 'It's about Nico's jewellery. She said once – well, not so long ago actually; God, I should have paid more attention. Only I never thought . . . How could I have imagined . . . ? Anyway she said – she made me promise – that if ever anything were to happen to her I would see to it that you received a piece of her jewellery in remembrance. Something personal, she said, something that was particularly hers. So . . . '

I had continued my battle with the gumboots, deliberately postponing the moment of victory: it gave me something to do while I was listening. Suddenly into my fumbling hands I found that William had thrust a small chamois leather bag containing what felt like miniature sweets.

'So I thought this . . . ' he muttered by way of explanation. 'Nico didn't have much jewellery of her own, so I thought this . . . these . . . That is, *we* thought, we all thought . . . that these would be perfect. They are aquamarines – part of a mixed bag of semiprecious stones her mother gave her for our wedding. They're just loose at present but you could have them set. Into a bracelet or something.'

He was lying. William was lying. He was such a bad liar, you could always tell; it was one of the most attractive things about him. Now, why should he be lying in a small private matter like this between the two of us? I looked up, right into his eyes, to see if I could spot the reason. Behind the overlay of acute discomfort there was nothing there but gentleness – I would almost call it fondness; tenderness anyway. So there could be only one explanation, and it did him credit: he was lying in order to rub a little ointment on my wounds. Because Nico had clearly never said to him anything of the kind. Once she had opted for the high jump she hadn't spared me a thought, either regarding jewellery or anything else. But William was going to maintain the fiction that she had. How sweet of him, how truly generous and thoughtful. He probably imagined, these stones being a gift from her mother, that Nico had been specially attached to them. No, he knew her too well to think that, but he probably thought I might think it and be pleased.

I loosened the string of the bag and poured out the contents into the palm of my hand. There were a dozen or so little pale blue gems, cut like lozenges. Very pretty; it was like holding the chippings from an iceberg. 'And Nico's mother knows you're giving them to me?' I asked. 'She doesn't mind?'

William almost jumped. 'Mind? Lord, no. No, God, no, of course not. It was her idea as well.' He shot me a look of anguish. 'The choice, I mean: she helped us make it.'

'I see,' I said, seeing in fact very little. And then a thought suddenly struck me. Wasn't it a bit odd that

Nico should have had these stones with her? Why on earth, when she hadn't bothered with clothes or reading matter, would she have travelled to Italy with a bag of miscellaneous gems she had no apparent need of, and couldn't even wear, seeing they were unset?

'Ah,' said William unhappily when I mentioned this. 'Yeah. Well. She didn't have them with her, of course. My ma brought them over.'

'Your mother? Specially? Specially brought them over? For me?'

Talk about shuffling, his feet were practically tap dancing. 'She . . . I . . . I asked her to. I wanted to have something to give you, see. A memento. Something tangible, concrete. I know it's silly but . . . '

I kissed him then. I couldn't help it. I was so touched, so moved to think that in those terrible early moments of bereavement he had actually thought of me, I clean forgot about embarrassment, both his and mine, and sprang up and threw my arms around him and kissed him.

The physical contact – probably, come to think of it, our first trunk contact ever – worked a brief wonder. For an instant everything seemed to go easier between us. Maybe it's a characteristic of the male – to find the short range easier to deal with than the middling, I don't know, my experience of these things is so slight – or maybe it's the absence of eye contact that does it, but in this new position, with us pressed together close as wrestlers, William's reserve seemed to vanish. 'Sarie,' he choked into my hair, using Nico's name for

111

me – another first. 'Oh, Sarie, help me. What a balls-up it is. I wish we could go back, how I wish we could go back.'

I made the mistake – or perhaps it wasn't a mistake – of prising myself away slightly in order to look at him. 'Help you how?'

He looked back at me blurrily, hardly seeming to understand the question. Then he quivered and his unease came back tenfold, and he leaped away from me and pointed a finger at the bag, unintentionally jabbing me quite hard in the stomach. 'By ac . . . ac . . . accepting those, is what I meant. Like I said, have them set; wear them. Go to Aspreys or wherever and have them properly set and . . . send me the bill.'

Send me the bill. Don't bring me the bill even, send it. The cut-off was as sudden as our coming together had been. Still, William had made such an effort in broaching the subject at all that I didn't feel hurt or repulsed by this truncated ending, rather the opposite, I felt oddly flattered by the whole proceeding. 'I'll keep you to your word,' I smiled. And he smiled back and made a sort of goldfish opening of the mouth that I think he intended as a kiss blown in my direction, and then he was off, leaving me still a prisoner of the wellies.

11

It was a long time, nearly three and a half years, before I saw William again. His conscience must have ground slowly, like the mills of God. But he had one, and grind it did, and in the end that's what matters.

We spoke over the phone a couple of times. I rang him to ask about a convenient day for picking up my stuff, and whether I could hang on to some of Nico's Shakespeare books until after the exams – a few odds and ends like that – and he rang me to tell me the date of the memorial service that was being held for Nico at Delham and to ask me if I needed transport there. All very friendly and civil. Please do. I'll bring them back. Don't bother, keep them – and by the way, good luck. Thanks, I'll need it. You'll be coming then – to the memorial do? Um, ah, definitely, if I can. Ollie's a sure starter, I'll give him a buzz if you like and fix a lift for you. Great – maybe a bit nearer the date? Yeah, right, it is a bit early still – we'll keep in touch. Yep, we'll keep in touch.

By which we meant we would do nothing of the kind, and we both knew it. I went round to collect my gear mid morning when I was certain William would be out, and I never heard any more from him about the service, so I assumed he had sensed my reluctance to attend it and had tactfully let the matter drop.

Plop, into the pool of the past. And who was I to blame him? Putting both Sherwoods from my mind became indeed a vital piece of my survival strategy. The future yawned before me like a mist-wrapped chasm over which was set a plank – narrow flat and grey. Where this plank led, there was no telling, all I could see looming out of the mist was the vague shape of the oncoming exams, and beyond that fuzzier shapes still. Possibly, granted I found a university willing to take me, and my parents agreed to pay the fees, a further period of study. If not, a job of some description. Sooner or later a job in any case. Then what? A career? A lover? Marriage? With my credentials? Anyway, whatever lay ahead, I knew I could only reach it if I edged my way along the plank gradually, step by step; like Orpheus, never looking back. One glimpse of the scintillating world I had inhabited so briefly with Nico – one flash of her smile, one shimmer of her ball gown – and my foot would falter and I would be unable to keep on my safe but dingy course.

All very well in theory, but when exam time came along this deliberate policy of forgetting was not so easy to stick to. At every session Nico's name was called out loudly by the invigilator. Some days even repeated. The first time, what with the full 'Nicolette' and the unfamiliar, little used Sherwood surname, it barely clicked with me, and when it did, it was only in a small part of my mind, the rest being already busy

114

with the question paper. But the next day and the next, and so on for the entire fortnight, it constituted a growing problem. How not to think of a polar bear, all over again. And that in itself was enough to set the memory wheels in motion. Polar bear; Arianna's little foible; Nico, Ollie and I picturing her indulging in it, so buoyed up on our own fizz we were hardly earthbound but seemed to float like astronauts in the capsule of the soft Italian summer night. Eventually I got round the difficulty by embracing Nico for the duration, and to hell with it. Dragging her with me through the papers and using her as a reference book. What was that quotation we said would impress the examiners? You know, the one from that German geezer, whatever he was called? That's the one. How do you spell his name? All those consonants – you sure? How did that other sonnet go – the one we said was kind of a mirror version of this? Remind me about that business of Charles Bovary and his patient: did the man die or did he just get worse? Is 'hibou' one of the x plurals? It worked: she soon got fed up and left me to my scribbling.

I was usually the last to hand in my paper. And even if I wasn't, I purposely lingered on in the classroom until the other candidates had left. They were all kids, and they all knew each other, and I felt cut off from them and ancient and ashamed. After I had done this a few times I began to notice another girl doing the same. Had she left with the rest I would never have spotted her as being what she was, namely a truly mature student, much more mature in all aspects than I was myself: she looked about thirteen. In fact the digits were correct but not the order, she was thirty one. It was practically the first thing she told me about herself – her age. How we got talking I don't remember, not the first approach, but it's a safe bet it was she, Angela, who made it. She was a top class icebreaker. In fact more than break, ice just melted away in her vicinity. If Scott had had her with him on his polar trek he'd have made it back to base camp without so much as a chilblain. I wouldn't be surprised if an archaeologist of the future, chancing on her remains, were to find an electric stove inside her to account for the warmth she gave out.

When first she turned its bars on me I instinctively balked, suspecting her of hollow, airhostessy cordiality and nothing more, but she didn't even notice my mean-spirited misgivings, she just beamed on regardless. 'Give a lung for that figure of yours,' she said admiringly, tilting her whole body sideways the better to size me up. 'You what, honey pot? *Twenny-five? Twenny-six?*'

Those months spent coursing after Nico had evidently taken their toll. I told her, tripping out the *t*'s in a way that already felt stilted, that I was twenty.

'Twent-ty,' she mimicked. 'That's chicken feed. Guess how old I am?' And leaving no time for a reply, 'I'm thirty. Man, no, thirty-one now; it's my birthday today. My friends all say it's a crap way to celebrate, sitting for your A-levels. Fact they say adult education is a crap idea altogether, but I tell them to go fry their eyeballs. Way I see it, it's life insurance. When my time's up and the Lord calls me, he'll say to Peter, Where's Angela? Fetch me Angela. And Peter will say, Hey, wait, Lord, sorry, You can't have Angela, not yet, she's still studying.'

In the re-telling it sounds tame enough, but you have to visualise the body language that went with it. And the body too for that matter – that padded rosy brown caddy of energy without a harsh line to be found on it anywhere. You have to picture to yourself the eyes constantly screwed up in amusement, the mouth twisting at the edges with self-mockery as it shuttles from side to side an ever present piece of chewing gum; see the hands, supple as fins, with their long curved fingernails, busy embellishing the spoken words with a rococo sign language of their own; and above all you have to hear the cascade of her laughter splashing over everything.

She laughed now and went on to ask me about which questions I'd answered, and ten minutes later we were still there chatting, and twenty minutes later we were outside in a café having coffee, and three weeks after the exams were over we were sharing a flat.

Well, a room, really, was all it was: a bed-sit with a doll-sized kitchen built into one corner, and a bathroom in the corridor outside that served six other people besides ourselves. All female – it was a strictly hen set-up, a roost for the working bird.

That's what I mean about the plank walk. If you keep edging along one step at a time, and don't look down or

117

back or get impatient, there's always space to put your foot. The plank sort of inches forward with you. Before the exams my main problem, far more pressing than whether I passed them or failed, had been where to go and live when they were done. My parents had been kind to me in the aftermath of Nico's death and had taken my return stoically, evincing hardly a flinch, but they were clearly shaken to their marrow by the idea of the arrangement being permanent. I would catch them looking at one another when they thought I wasn't watching, and exchanging glances of glum resignation shot with panic: they'd known the reprieve couldn't last forever. They had a life, I think, when I wasn't there; they must have done; a life in which they cheered one another up and did things together at weekends like golf and crosswords and hunting for antiques. They had a daughter too – that 'Sarah' they mentioned to people casually and in whose normality they tried to believe, but whose presence paradoxically made this impossible.

A daughter whom they *used* to mention to people, that is. After I had moved in with Angela I doubt they issued many more bulletins about my namesake's activities, and those they did would have been pretty vague. Yes, she's here in London studying for a degree. Maths, of all things. Such an arid subject, especially for a girl. Digs? Well, for the moment she's sharing with a . . . (No, they wouldn't have touched on the subject of Angela, the less said on that frizzy head, the better.) Well, for the moment she's found somewhere out Bayswater way. (Or Kensington Church Street way, or Holland Park way, they wouldn't have touched on Notting Hill Gate very willingly either.) *Rather* small, *not* quite the area one would have liked, but still . . . she's happy, and . . .

And they were temporarily freed from the burden Fate had laid upon their shoulders, it having slipped conveniently off again of its own accord. Did Angela, on the receiving end, know what she was getting? Not in all the furry detail, of course, but she had a pretty shrewd idea. She mused about it once quite openly. 'Posh little pixies like you,' she said, prodding me on the breastbone, 'Don't shack up with a fat black cashier my age unless there's something *seriously* wrong somewhere, now do they?'

But when I started to come clean and explain she prodded me again, this time into silence. 'Hold it, Twinkletoes. All I want to know is, it's natural, no? I mean, this fit or whatever it is comes over you – you were born that way, right? Well, then, it's natural, and what's natural's OK by me. You going to savage me or anything? No. Then unwind, forget about it, let's take the days as they come.'

'Homicidal maniacs are natural too, though,' I felt bound to point out. 'Hemlock's natural. So are earth-quakes.'

'Don't smartypant me. You know what I mean.'

I did. She meant she was my pal and would stand by me. Oh shit, if hearts could be bossed, how that would simplify matters. I would boss mine into belonging to

Angie and to her alone. I would return her loyalty, stay on, and together we would continue on the cosy, urban path she'd got mapped out for us. We'd go to teaching college and become teachers. Couple of unexciting, well-meaning, fairly competent Profs. Behind our backs our students, seeing us so close, would call us lesbians. Some of the staff members would do likewise. But we'd be that fond of each other, it wouldn't bother us a bit. So what, if we were? We'd do our shopping, our cooking, eat our scrambled eggs on the weekends in front of TW3, wash our hair, maybe put in the odd dyed streak as it got greyer, get mildly pissed on beer – do all the small solace-bringing things Angie was so good at, and muddle through the years that way. There were worse destinies by far. I would have the odd relapse, of course: go off for a few hours, come back looking a fright and miss work the next day. But unless it happened during prize-giving or some public occasion like that it wouldn't greatly matter. Angie would cover up for me, stuff my clothes into the washer without inspecting them too closely, and gradually the episodes would become fewer, and the phases in between longer, until one day they would just cease altogether. By the time I reached retirement age I might not even remember having had them.

Unless of course there was a repetition of the underground encounter. That might have altered the picture a bit. I don't know if I could have withstood another of those shocks without something in me snapping. As it was it took me months to find my feet again. It

happened during the evening rush hour. On the Picca-
dilly line. I was strap hanging and trying to read a logic
book at the same time. The train pulled into a station
and I was jolted forward so that I collided with a
woman who had this kid in tow holding an iced lolly.
The lolly spattered everywhere, and the woman started
protesting and the kid started whining and I started to
apologise – although it wasn't really my fault at all – and
then, I don't know why, perhaps just to distance myself
from all the fuss, my glance strayed to the platform
outside and in the river of jostling travellers, Zot! I saw
one of my own kind: a werewolf, the second in my
lifetime, the first since Nico. He was a middling-young
Hispanic looking creature with greasy ringlets and a
grubby overcoat but style to sink a fleet. I recognised
him straight away and let out a howl despite myself,
and straight away the whole public sphere – the train,
the station, the posters, the press of people, the whining
child, the clucking woman at my elbow – shrank to
the size of a bubble car holding just the two of us. Him
and me. His eyes and mine and the quivering current
connecting us.

There was so little time; the train was already
shuddering to depart. I flailed my arms around like a
person on the verge of drowning, cuffing whoever got in
my way, struggling to gain the exit. Behind me I heard
voices raised in indignation, and the mackintoshed arm
of some meddling busybody came down to bar my way.
I fear I may have bitten it because it was raised again
quickly to a chorus of more shouts. Tough luck on its

121

owner: no one was going to stop me reaching that plat-form. No one and nothing.

I slipped through the closing doors with a feeling of triumph: had I been an inch fatter or a second slower off the mark I'd never have made it. But the feeling soon died. As I wheeled round to check that my clothes were free and not caught in the jaws of the door, I saw him again. *In*side the carriage – now wasn't that symmetrical: he must have jumped on through another door at the exact moment I jumped off – pushing his way down the centre aisle in search of me, his head turning frantically from side to side. The passengers looked pretty nettled by now: for all I know they may have lynched him: I waited on the platform for an hour, and waited there again the same time every day for a week, but he never came back.

Good thing? Bad thing? Who can say? But it certainly felt bad at the time. Unsettling to the verge of uprooting.

Not that Angie didn't have problems of her own in the sentimental sphere. But they were not of the up-rooting kind, in fact they were the dead opposite: she got planted by her men friends time and time again, dumped in a hole and covered with earth and then trodden on and left to shoot potatoes. It was partly her fault: she *would* fall for such shits. They had to be young and they had to be beautiful, which meant, if they were going to even contemplate having an affair with her, they had to be shits by definition almost. I would quote her own wisdom back at her, 'Teenage male models aren't going to shack up with a fat black cashier your age unless there's something seriously wrong somewhere,' but in vain. She would grin and agree and swear she'd learnt her lesson, and then along another pretty shit would come, and off she'd go, rendering up her all to him on a platter; and after said shit had taken the bit he was interested in – plaff! – her matchless gift would be tossed aside and the horticultural process would be repeated.

Still, they gave us something to talk about, all these romantic upsets of Angie's. And among the other inmates of the hen coop they made her even more popular than she already was. All the world loves a jilted lover.

No, I'm being slick and unfair. It was not the case at all. By and large these lonely, struggling women, to whom life had given good reason to be sour and competitive, were a darn generous bunch. As demonstrated by their attitude towards me when out of the blue that early summer evening, two weeks before I was due to sit for my finals, William rang with his Cinderella invitation to the ball. All godmothers, not an ugly sister among them.

They were as mystified as I was myself, but far more excited. Who is this bloke, Sarah? How come you've never told us about him before? You ashamed of your posh past? You don't need to be: no one can help the way they're born. Could be a king even, wouldn't matter. Long as he isn't a pervert or Jack the Ripper or someone; long as he isn't going to mess up your life, barging into it again after all this time. What d'you mean, you used to be close? How close? Close how? You two cosy up on a school bench and swap logarithms, or what? A *widower*? You're joking? The husband of your best friend? Oh, God, that explains it. The mourning's over and now he's looking for a . . . God, girl, this is serious! We've got to get you looking good, but really, really good, and that means . . .

Pause and weighty silence: the enormity of the task evidently flummoxed them. With no Nico to keep me up to the mark I had indeed let myself go badly from the grooming angle. Waxing, tweezing, manicures – I hadn't bothered with any of these. Somehow there had seemed no point. A few stray hairs never stopped anyone solving a maths problem: look at those mustachios of Descartes.

. . . What do you say we begin with weeding out some of those eyebrows?

I gave myself over passively to their care, only rousing myself briefly now and then to squeal, and/or assert a right of veto over the use of Carmen rollers. I have a slightly Red Indian look about me and my hair is best left straight: whoever heard of a curly squaw? Their ministrations seemed to take forever: I was stripped, peeled, washed, dried, creamed, pummelled; following which I was wrapped in a bath robe and plumped into a chair with my head tipped back and tweezed and coiffed and painted; then I was stood up again and dressed in someone's lacy Marks and Sparks nightie – one of the very few floor length garments in our joint possession – stripped again in favour of a robe someone

124

else wore for singing in the chorus at concerts, and stripped again, and again re-dressed. This time in a caftan of Angie's, made of saffron silk. When they had finished, and I'd been doused with scent and topped off with a pair of clip-on earrings, I was led to the landing – the only place where there was a mirror long enough to reflect me whole – and bidden to look at the result.

Now, I am not vain, I defy anyone to be vain who'd just been through the humbling process I'd been through, but I have to admit I looked quite special. Better than I have ever looked in my life, before or since. A Maya priestess, say, or a Guatemalan icon. Not that I've ever seen either, but they give the idea. Exotic anyway. Arresting, an enemy would probably have called me; a friend might have gone as far as stunning. The clips were two huge clusters of pearls, and they garnished my face like earmuffs. Beautiful I shall never be, pretty neither, the wolf strain is far too strong, but that evening I swear I came close to being both. I don't like the word, with its overtones of bars and cages, but I think what best describes me was 'captivating'.

William seemed to think so at any rate, although to be fair his various strands of thought must have been in a terrible tangle by then, enough to ensnare anyone. What to say. How much. How to say it without looking either mean or feeble or both. Whether indeed to say it at all, and not just cop out again and run. He blinked as I walked down the stairs to meet him, and in a theatrical gesture that came oddly from him, raised his forearm and rubbed a wrist into his eye. It may of course have been the unfamiliar surroundings that fazed him: I doubt he'd ever been to the area before, or seen the inside of a boarding house, not one like this. Or it may have been all those pairs of female eyes ogling at him through the banisters, or it may have been the contrast between the dark of the hallway and the brightness of my *mise*. But I tend to think it was just me, this new and resplendent Sarah, who on the outside looked so strange and different, and yet who on the inside would have felt to him as familiar and comfortable as a much worn pair of slippers. Slippers, what was more, with happy memories attached to them: telly supper slippers, mucking-around-in slippers, slippers chosen by Nico and to whose fabric some trace of her still clung. No effort was necessary with me, no barriers needed crossing, I slotted back smoothly into his life without so much as a click.

'Whatcher doing in that dump, solicitor's daughter?'

I told him about the maths and then waited for his laughter, but it didn't come.

Instead I got a pat on the hand. 'Srewth,' he murmured, 'you're a funny creature.' Then he switched on the ignition and said no more, merely kept up a low tuneless whistling noise as he concentrated on his driving. He liked driving and did it well. The car was a low slung sports car, new and growly and flashy, and drew the envious attention of other motorists whenever we stopped at a traffic light.

I enjoyed this, and I could tell by the growing chirpiness of his whistling that William enjoyed it too.

Showing off – I'd almost forgotten what it was called. It surprised me how easy we were in each other's company. Nico sat there between us, perched on the handbrake, her shoulders practically rubbing against ours; but instead of it filling us with pain and causing us to retract, as it had done earlier when the wounds were fresh, her presence united us. I could almost feel her working at the task: physically pulling us together. Go on, be pals again, the pair of you, be buddies, or do I have to sing you Auld Lang Sodding Syne? It was the first time since her death that I could hold her in my head in a simple, non-friction fashion, without some other part of me fighting against it.

'She'd have liked tonight,' William said, in an eerie kind of footnote to my thoughts, as we drove westward over the Chiswick flyover. He used no preamble – he knew it wasn't necessary. 'This friend of mine who's giving the party tonight, she approved of him. Said he knew how to live, I don't know why.' He went back to his whistling for a while and then ventured, 'Maybe it's the house.'

'Why, what's with the house?'

'What's *with* the house? What a way to talk. Nothing's *with* the house. At least . . . well, you'll see for yourself when we get there. It's sort of farmy, I guess you'd call it. A de luxe farmhouse. But with pictures . . . oh, pictures . . . ' Sigh, and after another mile or so on the clock, 'Or maybe it's the gardens – there are acres of those.' Five more miles, could even have been ten, 'The freedom, you know.'

I knew.

Tuh *tuuh* tuh tuh tuh, tuh-tuh-tuh-*tuh*-tuh. The whistle was still tuneless, but the rhythm was unmistakably that of the Doggie in the Window.

I prised Nico's foot off the gear lever and laid my hand on his. 'Oh, Will.'

'Oh, Sarah,' he echoed.

After this we spoke no more, in fact once we had arrived at the dance we lost sight of each other almost straight away and didn't meet up again until later, when the crowd had thinned and people had begun to emerge from the scrum as individuals and not mere dots of colour on a Pointillist's canvas. William parked the car alongside that of some crony of his and they strolled off together, leaving me to make my way into the house alone. Not that I minded. I was wrapped in a mysterious cloud of contentment. I felt beautiful and safe and totally at ease in this unknown place. Quite why, I wasn't able to say. Perhaps it was because before, as a satellite in Nico's orbit, lit by her sun, I had been to some extent visible to these people, whereas now I was invisible and could happily go back to my favourite role of spectator. Those few faces that were familiar to me from earlier days, after a little frown of puzzlement, glanced through me as if I were a ghost.

A glamorous ghost, though, that much the faces, both male and female, couldn't help betraying. Angie's caftan might have been non-regulation but it knocked all those bouffant lampshade concoctions out of the ring. And in my guise of glamorous ghost I wafted through the rooms noting and enjoying everything: the pictures, the furniture, the ornaments, the marquee ballroom straight out of Fragonard, the throng of guests that filled it (straight out of the Tatler, these, plus a few out of Gotha as well: there was a light peppering of younger Royals), the tapestries, the sculptures, the vases of flowers set in every window recess, the vistas onto the floodlit gardens beyond – the whole exquisite pageant.

'Farmhouse' even 'de luxe' was hardly an accurate description: I can only think William gave it on account of the ceilings, which were perhaps a foot or so lower than the ones he was accustomed to. But with regard to the paintings he was spot on: they were to sigh for and die for. It was like having a private ticket to the Hermitage, with no time restrictions and no curator to say, Move on, or, Don't go so close, or, Stand aside so that other visitors can have a look. There were no other visitors. The older guests sat or stood, backs to the wall, ingesting drink and smoke and scandal, and salmon mousse and strawberries from the buffet; the younger ones flitted past oblivious, each following some trail of pheromones and laying more in their wake. Watching them all – dispassionately like you would watch a bee-hive through a sheet of glass or an ant hill in someone else's garden – I realized for the first time in my life what parties at this level of society were about. They weren't about fun and relaxation, those could be better procured on a yacht or a grouse moor or in the south of

France; no, they were more like industrial fairs – places to display your wares, sample other people's, sniff out the competition, foil it where possible, make useful contacts, up-date your technology, expand your market. No wonder there was such a glow of perspiration on all the participants' faces: it wasn't the heat or the excitement or the dancing, it was the sheer hard work.

And no wonder they none of them paid attention to me: they had gone through the list of exhibitors carefully beforehand – that was an important part of the job, scanning the field, knowing who was who and where they belonged and how much they counted – and I was simply not on it. My name like Ulysses's was Nemo. To all but one or two old party pros, who seeing me alone and available sidled up and asked me to dance, I was nobody. And even to them . . . well, judging by the please-yourself shrugs with which they took my refusal, I doubt they were much interested in my identity.

But then, in the after-midnight lull when the pace had slowed and the music with it, William and I met up again and he began to dance with me; and in his arms, perhaps on account of the protective way they held me, wrapping me round like bean shoots do a pole, or perhaps on account of the length of time they held me – dance after dance after dance – I gradually became visible again. As we passed them I could see other couples on the floor eyeing us and then whispering to one another in a quizzing sort of way, Who's that bird Sherwood's got hold of? Looks like they're pretty pally. Where's he been keeping her? Why is it we haven't seen her around before? Face is vaguely familiar. Foreign, do you suppose?

Was it actually while we were dancing that William hit on the neat solution to his problem? I think it must have been. I think it was the friendly way our bodies fitted together that decided him. That and the drink – the Dutch courage I am always so ready to ascribe to him, seeing he was so short on any other kind. I can picture the inside of his head – the thoughts, loose, blurry, running into one another the way watercolours do when the paper is too wet: Should tell her; right thing to do; brought her here on purpose, can't back out now; but not just yet; bit later maybe; maybe in the car; calls for a bit of privacy, thing like this; can't just say . . . Or can I? Should I? Yes, I should; right thing to do; brought her here on purpose . . .

Thoughts spinning, head spinning, body spinning slightly too as we revolve slowly clockwise to the strains of Only You. The whole thing is faintly uncomfortable, since his conscience is prickling all the while. And then suddenly: *Ahhh*. Relief, peace, as he chances on a balm. The spinning stops, the thoughts come into focus – one, particularly, in the foreground. Why not? It would solve everything. Loneliness, randiness, maternal goadings to remarry and produce an heir, the bother of finding someone suitable and the bother of housekeeping in the interim – all set to rights with one simple manoeuvre. Simple? Well, simple compared to the alternative. And speaking of the alternative, no need any more to do anything about it. Abracadabra and it would vanish;

leaving no trace, seeing that the object – that wretched little blob of mineral that was causing all the fuss – would go to the right person automatically.

That's how I imagine it went, give or take a few details.

'Sarah, funny little Sarah. You smell so nice. Why don't we go outside for a moment and get a breath of fresh air?'

Quite the romantic. We loosened our grip of one another and wandered hand in hand through the suite of rooms like a pair of zombies until we reached a door that led onto the gardens. People spoke to us on the way – they did to William at any rate – but he brushed past them without a word, keeping his head well down and ploughing forward with me in tow, so that it seemed it was his nose that was cutting a path for us.

I had a fair idea of what was coming – i.e. some sort of physical advance on William's part – so I had to think hard and fast about that nose. Nico had managed it, but could I? It wasn't so much the full-blown sexual act – knowing William, it would be a long time before we got round to that – it was the kissing, the tender-ness, the effusions. Could I convincingly snog with a man with a nose like that? Our bodies fitted OK, that was true, but would our faces fit?

'What do you think? Can I handle it? Can I take him seriously as a lover?' I asked Nico, whom I had had the presence of mind to drag behind me at the last moment. Strung out like that, the three of us made quite a little procession.

But for some reason the question seemed to rile her, even worse than those I had asked her in the exam room, and with a tug of her hand she slipped my grasp and was gone, leaving me alone with William and my doubts.

It didn't come to kissing, though. I was surprised: the approach William made was much more stately. I'd been expecting a tipsy lunge in the dark; what I got was both much, much more and at the same time, in a way I couldn't quite pinpoint until the reason became clear to me, much less.

He led me around on a zigzag course until he had found the place he was looking for: a walled garden within the garden, darker and warmer and altogether more private, with a sunken area in the middle, right in the centre of which there was a sundial set about by dog roses. He had given a sundial to Nico, I remembered: perhaps he had a thing about them.

'This is a moondial,' he said, as if to correct me. It was the second time that evening that he had seemed to hear my thoughts before I had voiced them. He sounded very melancholy, and my heart went out to him. (A funny metaphor, that, but I like it; it explains exactly how I felt: as if my heart had stretched out a little further than I'd been prepared to do myself and drawn him close.) It occurred to me fleetingly that if I'd had a brother this was more or less how I would have wanted him to be.

'Look,' he said, 'I'll show you how it works. Come here, stand just there, that's right.' And he led me towards the little column and, placing me opposite him, took my hand in his and guided my forefinger over the face of the dial. 'Feel these rings,' he said. 'Feel how they swivel. If you line them up datewise they give you the exact phase of the moon. This one was built for a gardener a couple of centuries ago – to tell him when to plant things. I gave one to Nico once. Had it copied from this. It was the only present of mine she ever really liked.'

'Oh, yes, I remember,' I said. 'I read about it in a mag. That was before I met you, though. Either of you. Only the article said it was a sundial.'

'Nope,' he said, and kept silent for a while, watching me. 'Moondial was what it was. But tonight there's no need for a moondial, is there? Tonight . . . ' He glanced skywards, and I saw his Adam's apple jerk as if he had swallowed something bulky: I reckon that was the moment he decided to take the plunge. 'Tonight she's new – a brand new Moon Goddess. Let's see if she'll grant my wish.' And leaning abruptly forward he took my face in his hands, clamping the earrings rather painfully on each side, tilted it so that the light from the pale sickle moon fell straight on it, and said, very faintly, very fast, so that, what with covered ears and the rustling of leaves and the throb of the band in the distance, I wasn't sure for a second if I had heard him correctly: 'I wish you would marry me. Would you marry me, Sarah – please?'

Unlike mine, William's face was in shadow. How did I know then, after just the briefest pause for reflection, that this was indeed a serious, bona fide proposal of marriage he had just made to me and not a mere joke? It must have been his voice – the urgency in his tone. Or the way his hands trembled, shaking the pearl earrings until they rattled in my eardrums like canker in a cat's. Or else it was the deep intake of breath after the 'please', as if he was storing up with oxygen to tide him over until I had given my reply. Oh yes, there was no doubt about it: he was serious all right. Hard though it was to credit, he was utterly serious and so was the offer.

But what should my reply to it be? Well, as regards the 'should', I suppose I knew already, deep down. What I didn't know, and what caused me to hold my breath in suspense along with William, was what my reply *would* be. Because it could so easily dodge the censor in me and pop out unvetted. I felt a bit like I imagine Jesus must have felt on that mountaintop with the devil: bewildered and scared and tempted and excited all at once. There it lay: my patch of world. Far smaller than the one the devil had been brokering, OK, but still not to be turned down lightly: security; goodies galore; two beautiful houses; a title that would instantly change my name from Nemo to whatever the Latin was for Somebody, and Somebody Quite Prominent at that; an income that would free me from my parents and vice versa and guarantee I never had to work unless I chose to; in short, a fairytale heap of advantages on the material plane.

And not only on the material plane: I would also

have this kind, good, generous, tender-hearted man as my companion. Agreed, he had a weak character and a mum as fierce as Genghis Khan to make up for it, but I knew this about him already, so there would be no nasty surprises in store. And he on his side knew – perhaps not all about me, but enough to prevent me feeling I was doing him wrong, should I accept him. He'd been married to Nico after all: a werewolf wife was no novelty. In fact it could even be he had singled me out for this very reason. From a sense of nostalgia.

'Yes, Nico, for the sake of Auld Lang Sodding Syne, and what's wrong with that?' She was back again, sitting cross-ankled on the moondial, slap between me and William, cutting him off from me entirely: her astral form or whatever it's called gave her a lot of spatial leeway, it seemed it could balance on almost anything. She looked a bit put out. It struck me it might be jealousy.

However it struck me wrong. She didn't speak, but her features, unlike William's, were undimmed by the shadow, and that half-smiling mouth of hers and those burning golden eyes, more like a wolf's than ever, seemed to be telling me a lot of things, all with generous intent. Don't make my mistake, Sarie, they seemed to be saying. Don't think you can knuckle down and settle just for fondness and a cushy pad. It's not enough, believe me, it's not enough. And it's not *far* enough either. Your heart has the travel plans; you must let it do the driving. Who do you love? Who do you really love? Who, when you see them, makes your

136

heart race? Who, when you think of them, makes you smile inside? Who would you follow to prison in order to be with? Who, when you think of losing them, makes you feel you'd rather die? If you haven't met up with anyone like that yet, then hold on till you do. Don't be fobbed off with second best: ask life for the tops. And when you get it, then go for it for all you're worth.

Ironic that she should be the one to tell me this. Didn't she know she was my tops and there would never be another to replace her? And wasn't she aware of how bitterly she had disappointed me, ratting on me like that without a word and leaving me to live on in an empty world without her?

Apparently not, judging by the unconcerned way she sat there, swinging her feet and proffering the sort of philosophy tips you get inside a Christmas cracker. Apparently not. But banalities are sometimes true. No, often true. No, maybe almost always true: people are as snobbish about the commonplace as they are about common accents, but that doesn't alter its value. Nico's advice was in no way original maybe, but it was sound. She spoke from experience. If I married William – well, maybe I wouldn't go and dive off a bridge to my death like she had done: that was too extreme a reaction for a circumspect creature like me – but I wouldn't be happy, not completely, not for long. Always, in the midst of the plush and the pamperedness and the politeness, I would feel something was missing. It was cussed of me, and it was cussed of life, but that was they way it was.

And then there was the nose.

'Oh, William, forgive me . . . It's a lovely idea and I'm touched, I really am . . . But I couldn't. I mean, I can't. I mean, sorry, no, I won't. It would never work – you know that as well as I do.'

I could see his face more clearly now, though, in some way I can't quite describe, the Nico of my imagining was still placed there between us. (Perhaps her astral body had turned see-through in the meantime.) He looked . . . well, he looked . . . not in any way downcast, as you might expect of a rejected suitor, he looked more taken aback. Taken aback and puzzled and a little bit affronted as well. He let go of me abruptly and took a step backwards. 'What do you mean, it wouldn't work? Of course it would work – that's the one thing we need have no doubt about: that it would work. We've tried each other out; we've lived under the same roof, for god's sake; we've seen each other day after day at breakfast; we know darn well we don't get on each other's nerves. And that's more than most couples know about each other when they get married.'

'But there's a lot of things we don't know; that we haven't tried.'

His voice turned knowing. 'Ah, so it's sex,' he said. 'You're worried about the sex. Are you still a virgin, little Sarie? Nico told me once you were a virgin.'

I wasn't quite sure how to reply to this. Mainly because I wasn't sure if I was still a virgin or not. Angie had arranged my deflowering for me with the help of a volunteer cousin – she said it wasn't natural at my age never to have had a man, and 'natural' had the force of a commandment in her vocabulary. But the process had remained open ended. Luther and I – that was the cousin's name: Luther – had spent a sticky afternoon together, tussling around on Angie's sofa-bed, which was that much wider than mine, but I had felt no pain and seen no blood, and had felt very little pleasure either, and when I'd asked Luther why this was he had shrugged his glistening mahogany shoulders and said, 'I guess it's because you try too hard. You want to learn to relax a bit, then you'll take to it fine. Don't worry.' And he'd chuckled, and with a 'Phew!' and a mop of his forehead climbed back into his jeans. Was that the postscript to a job well done or an admission of defeat? I never did discover. Might have been either or might have been neither – just a reaction to the heat: that day was stifling. Angie seemed satisfied afterwards with my naturalness, such as it now was, so I left it at that.

Anyway, technicalities aside, 'No' seemed the more honest answer to William's question.

He greeted this with an 'Oh'. A very neutral Oh, no inflexion to it at all. 'I see. So it's not sex then, I thought it was.'

'No, it's not sex,' I confirmed. And it wasn't, either: by then I was beginning to think I could quite fancy him. *In* the dark.

'I see,' he said again. (It's odd how often people say this when what they mean is quite the opposite: I do it sometimes myself.) 'Then what is it? There's some other man – that right? You've got someone else?' He stepped forward again and, without warning, his fist came down on the moondial. Hardish, though it seemed to leave Nico quite unmoved. 'What a fool I've been to leave it so long. What a bloody fool. Of course you've got someone else. I don't know why I ever thought . . . Except that I did: I thought . . . No, that's the trouble: I didn't think. I just let the days slip by without doing or thinking anything. What a fool. What a lazy, conceited fool.'

This show of emotion had a complicating effect on me. I realised that not only was I still tempted by William's offer but the temptation was a good deal stronger than before: if he was that miffed by my refusal, he evidently felt more deeply about me than I had thought. Oh dear. The houses, the perks, the goodies, the companionship, lit now by a ray of what appeared to be genuine affection – I could see all these desirable things drifting away from me, getting smaller and smaller by the second as if I were viewing them from the porthole of a departing spacecraft. Yet they were still within reach: all I had to do was change my mind, invert the route, say Yes, and there they would be again, mine for the taking.

'There isn't anyone else,' I heard someone say. It was a moment before I realised it was me. Or at any rate a part of me – that part that was greedier and therefore more easily bamboozled.

'There isn't? Are you sure?'

I smiled at the absurdity of this question but William didn't. 'Well,' I said, 'pretty sure. I mean – it's the sort of thing I ought to know about, no?'

'Of course,' he agreed earnestly, peering at me over the dial. (Was it the moonlight that was making him look so wan? No, I think it was his conscience gnawing into him again.) 'But if there's no one else, then I don't understand: why not me? Why turn me down? What's wrong with me? Do you find me that repulsive? Surely you don't want to go on living in that mole hole, do you, with all those worthy lady moles? Surely I can offer you something better than that?'

Absolutely, he could. My greedy part was getting uppish now: I could feel going on inside me the shuttling movement of an authentic tug-of-war. This way, that way, backwards and forwards, lapping the victory line. Say yes. Say no. Say yes. Say no. It was like being got at by touts – not a nice feeling at all.

William seemed well aware of my dilemma. A hat trick of thought reading, but so easy this time it hardly counted. 'No need to get into such a state, my little maths boffin,' he said, cupping my face again but only with his fingertips, as gentle as could be. 'Think it over. Take your time. It was selfish of me to rush things like that. Let's go back to square one again and pretend I've just asked you to marry me, but you haven't given me your answer. OK?

I had opened my mouth to say it was not OK – I knew I must refuse again immediately if I was not to lose out to Greedy Girl entirely – but he moved his fingers over my lips to hush me. 'No, don't say anything, not yet. *I'll* tell you what you say: you say, "William, that is a lovely idea but it has taken me by surprise and

141

I need a bit of time to get used to it. Do you mind if I give you my answer . . . " And then you set your own date. Tomorrow, Monday, Tuesday, whenever you like.'

'As long as it's not *too* long,' he amended, before removing his hand. He looked so sweet and pleading I hardly saw the nose at all. And then he put his head on one side, so that I saw it again, and said, 'Well?' And the lines that he had prepared for me, and that I was just about dutifully to recite, came out exactly as before: as a point blank refusal.

At this, William seemed to go to pieces, and not only as a figure of speech: he seemed literally to lose height, almost to crumple. 'Then that's it,' he said dejectedly and, backing away from the moondial, slumped down in a sitting position on the surrounding wall and let out a string of swearwords – limp like himself. 'Shit, blast, bugger, bother, hell. Nothing for it. I hoped I wouldn't, but I'll just have to tell you now.'

'Tell me what?' I was baffled, almost alarmed by his sudden change of mood. I shot a glance at the moondial to see if Nico could enlighten me, but she had gone of course: she was never around when I needed her.

'Tell you all. Confess. Spit out the whole squalid truth and have done with it. You don't think much of me already, judging by how nippy you were just now in turning me down: you might as well despise me outright.'

'Don't talk like that, Will,' I began. His abjection distressed me. 'I would never despise you. You are not the sort of person . . . '

But he cut me short. 'Oh yes, you would,' he said, 'And oh yes, you will, and oh yes, I am. Wait until you hear what I've done.'

'Why, what have you done? Can't be that bad, surely?'

He gave a rueful giggle. 'No, not that bad. Just petty. Come and sit over here a sec and I'll show you something.' And he pulled me down beside him, fished in his pocket and held up a small shiny object. In the semi-darkness it was hard to make out what it was. 'Remember this? This was to have been your engagement ring. Our engagement ring. Do you recognize it?'

I looked at it more closely: it was the topaz and diamond ring Nico had been wearing the night I first met her. The poison ring – the beautiful antique Italian one. 'Yes,' I said, 'I recognize it.'

He took my hand and slipped the ring on my finger. 'No strings attached, alas, no engagement, no marriage, no nothing, but anyway . . . its yours now. There!' And he gave a great puff of relief. 'I should have given it to you ages ago. Nico wanted you to have it. It was . . . ' He halted and the next words came out slowly, as if they needed forcing. 'It was this, you see – this was the piece of jewellery she made me promise I'd give you in the event of her death.'

I should have felt elated at this news but for some reason I just felt fuddled and sad. It didn't seem to make much difference now whether Nico had remembered me or not in her last days, or what she had done. It was all so long ago. 'Not the aquamarines, then?'

'No, not the aquamarines. They were a substitute. To make up for not giving you the ring. It wasn't a question of value – please don't think that, not even for a moment – it was more . . . Well, the idea, you see, was not to split the set. The parure, as the man from Christie's calls it. It's been in the family for generations now: the first Marquess bought it for his bride when they were on honeymoon in Italy; it was said to have belonged to Lucrezia Borgia . . . '

'*What*?' As the implications of William's confession sank in, I felt my mood lighten and brighten until it reached helium level. 'You mean . . . ? No, this needs spelling out to me. You mean you were prepared to go through with it and actually *marry* me, rather than split a set of jewellery? I don't believe that's possible. Nobody in their right mind does a thing like that. It's plain dotty.'

William started laughing too. Slightly shamefacedly. 'Wasn't my only reason,' he said. 'Still think it might have worked out well between us, but there. In fact, to tell the truth, it wasn't my reason at all: I don't give a shit for those old Borgia baubles, never did, never have done. They were probably a tourist con anyway; probably made in Naples in Seventeen Whatever and flogged to my ancestor at triple their value.'

'I know that wasn't the reason,' I said. 'It was your mum, wasn't it? Oh, Will, that's worse; it's dottier still: you were going to marry me, not in order not to split the set, but in order to *avoid telling your mum* that you were splitting the set. That's sheer lunacy.'

144

'No, it isn't. It's miserable cowardice. Congratul-ations, Sarie: you're well shot of me. And now . . . ' He got to his feet and turned away from me to take a last look at the moondial, 'I reckon I've grovelled enough: it's time I took you back to that ghastly doss-house. Think of me kindly sometimes, won't you, when you wear your ring.'

12

It's unbelievable how long it took me. I have a vague
memory, probably gleaned from some textbook on
economics (economists love using everyday objects
like that: pins, cans, jackets), of this man who owned a
sardine tin inside which he and everyone else believed
was enclosed a pearl of enormous worth. According
to the author, as long as the tin remained unopened it
made no difference on the financial plane whether the
pearl was there or not: to all practical ends the can
owner was a millionaire.

Was that what I was doing, then, when on returning
from the party I put the ring away in my spongebag,
classing it as unsuitable for my present life or indeed
for any future life I could see myself leading, and
thought no more about it? Was it my subconscious
trying to preserve my riches for me by not tapping
them or even raising the question whether or not they
were there to be tapped? Possible, but it didn't feel
like that at the time. (Well, it wouldn't, stupid. That's
the whole point about the subconscious: that it inter-
venes to shortcut your feelings.) I know, I know, but it
still didn't feel like that, not even when, a full month
later the thought finally came to me. It didn't creep

into my mind hangdog as if under sentence of recent banishment, it blitzed in on me like a revelation. Like a flash, a sudden flare of white-hot light. One moment I was lolling there on the sofa-bed, bored and aimless, going through the job offers column in search of some form of temporary employment to tide me over till the exam results were published, and the next my brain was in frazzles. The ring! She put it in the ring! That's what she did. Oh, why didn't I think of it earlier? Nico put her message in the ring!

So, no, I exclude the sardine tin theory entirely. I didn't dither, I didn't do any sitting around on any figurative fences: I was so impatient to get at that spongebag I practically dived off the bed, still horizontal. And when I'd got my hands on the bag I didn't fumble, didn't hesitate, didn't stop to think for an instant: What if there is? What if there isn't? I just tore open the zip, grabbed the ring, flipped it open, drew out the little screw of paper that was inside, flattened it on my palm and read what was written.

Flat B, 93 Chalmers Gardens, London W.9. It wasn't a letter; it was just an address, carefully printed out in Nico's handwriting. But that didn't matter: it was *the* address, the one the Frenchman had handed her on the train. I knew this straight away and with utter certainty: the railway ticket would have been too thick to fit into the cavity, so Nico had copied out the address for me on this tiny scrap of tissue paper. I folded my fingers over it and all I could think was how strange it was that this miniscule string of signs should set off such an avalanche of joy. Because that is the only way I can describe the flood of sensation that now came over me: as an avalanche. It left me no time for raising questions, still less hopes. I didn't ask myself: What is this place, I wonder? Why did Nico want me to go there? Did she go there herself without telling me? Was that where she went instead of to the dentist? If I go there will I learn anything more about her death? Or about her life, even? No, I simply felt happy again, the way I had been when she was alive and we were together. The intervening years, the pain, the loneliness, the plodding – all were swept aside in an instant and borne away from me, faster and faster and farther and farther until they were lost to sight and all I could make out was the shape of the dull, grey, narrow plank surfing after them like a runaway ski.

Farewell, little plank. Whatever lay ahead was not going to be boring. Tracking down the address, finding out who lived there, listening to whatever he or she or it might have to tell me about Nico – these things might be difficult, might be painful, might even be scary, but they wouldn't be boring, that was for sure.

Although my first sight of Dr Lestrange did, I admit, set me doubting for an instant. Despite his name, he was so ordinary. The house was so ordinary. Since childhood I had met scores of fusty, legal people – colleagues of my father's, guests at my parents' dinner parties – and this man seemed to be just another such. Grey hair, rimless glasses, a dark suit, a blue and white striped shirt, a pair of clean-shaven cheeks lapping over its stiff white collar, their rosy colour formed not by health but by a network of tiny broken veins; a waiting room stocked with rubber plants and geographical magazines; a beige-carpeted study with a big leather-topped desk and a pile of papers on it lit by a green-shaded reading light – a more conventional set-up you'd be pushed to find.

Dr Lestrange, as he sat there observing me over the polished surface of the desk, even had his fingers joined under his nose in a steeple point. The only dissonant note was sounded when instead of, 'Well, young lady, and what can I do for you?' or some bland opening like that, he reached forward, flashed the light abruptly into my face, stared into it intently for some seconds and then leant back again in his chair with a grunt. 'Can't be too careful,' he said. 'Had a lady in here the other week convinced I was an analyst. Freudian, if you please. Don't know who sent her. It could have been a mistake, of course, but equally it could have been a security check on my methods. They do things like that nowadays; spring things on you; they learnt it from the Michelin Guide.' He made a wriggling movement that seemed to draw all the parts of his body closer together; even the network of veins darkened as if suddenly contracted. 'But they won't trip me up that way,' he added a touch defensively. 'No, indeed. Stale, maybe, but sloppy, never. Now, let's see: we have established that you are a bona fide client, but who sent you, I need to know? For our files, you understand. How did you get wind of me?' He picked up a pencil, leant over the desk again and tapped me on the nose. 'Certainly not with that inadequate appurtenance.' And he laughed.

It was more of a chuckle, really. A professional man's professional chuckle – very little mirth in it and no warmth at all. 'Don't look alarmed,' he said. 'It's just my way of lightening the atmosphere. We've got serious business ahead of us, true, but there's no need to go about it in a funereal spirit. Quite the reverse, quite the reverse: if anything I look on myself more as a midwife. Now . . . ' And he tilted the light towards me again, although not right into my eyes this time, 'Please pay attention: I am about to ask who your sponsor is. Or was. By that I mean the person who referred you to this address. You will not, I stress *not*, give me their name – we prefer to preserve anonymity on that count: you may notice I have purposely not asked you for your own – but you will give me as full a physical description of them as you are able to furnish. Age, sex, height, weight, shape, skin colour, hair colour, eye colour and so forth. Any distinguishing feature, any mark or mole or blemish, on any part of the anatomy whatsoever, is of course a bonus, and very helpful for identification purposes, and I encourage you to give it. You may rely on my total discretion. So. Please. Off you go: describe to me your sponsor.'

He reeled all this off automatically, but it didn't matter. To me the invitation rang sweeter than, 'have a pot of caviar', or, 'have a free case of champagne'. Nico had been missing from my mind for so long that it was a treat to talk about her to anyone even remotely prepared to listen. I shut my eyes in order to have a nice blank screen to work on, and let the memories seep back in. At first they came in the form of rather stilted black and white photographs, similar to those I had chanced on in the papers before I met her – but then came the Delham portrait, coloured and life-size and far more detailed, and then her mirror image that first night of the ball, and then finally she herself breezed in a hundred different quick-change versions: reckless, studious, cold, drunk, hilarious, happy, weepy, cross, exhausted; in jeans, in an oilskin, in a bathrobe, in pyjamas, in the buff; dancing, quarrelling, flirting, gargling, doing the cross-word, stuffing herself with Marmite sandwiches . . . Nothing to do with the waiflike silhouette of the rose garden: this was Nico in cinemascope, or in 3D without the interference of those clumsy green and red specs.

Once I'd got started I could have gone on indefinitely. I kept remembering more and more details. The furry blond V on the nape of her neck when she put her hair up, and the way it tapered down the top of her spine. The mole on her ribcage – the heart-shaped one that the dermatologist wanted to see removed and William didn't. The thin white scar of a needless appendix operation: 'My mother said I could never go Brazil with her unless I had it out. So I did, but then I never went anyway.'

It must have been even more than Dr Lestrange had bargained for. He held up a pudgy, well-manicured hand to stop the flow. 'Thank you,' he said, 'that's ample. Normally at this point I go and check in our records, but in this case I think it is unnecessary: I remember the client in question, I remember her very clearly.' His gaze strayed towards the ceiling and his voice lost some of its professional detachment, became gentle, almost dreamy. 'In a desk job like this it's not every day that . . . No, it's not every day. Not at that age anyway, and not with all those gifts. So firm about it too. Never a waver. Most clients dither about for months.' He wriggled again, and again the movement seemed to have that rustling together, sheepdog effect on the various parts of his being. 'Ah well,' he resumed in a more businesslike tone, and peered at me over his glasses, 'Let's come back to you now. Do you know which way you are going to go? Or are you still in the wibbly-wobbly, one-foot-here-one-paw-there phase?'

My heart was pounding: Nico had been here, sat in the chair in which I was sitting. What had she come for? What had passed between her and Dr Lestrange? I longed to ask, but something warned me not to. The doctor was a cagey man; despite the appearance of normality he was running a cagey show: if he didn't even keep a record of his patients' names there was little hope he would divulge information about them, especially to a newcomer like myself. I wasn't sure, I said truthfully, in fact I wasn't really sure what I was doing here at all. I had simply come along because my friend – or my sponsor, if he preferred – had left me the address three years ago, shortly before committing suicide, and for various reasons there was no need to go into, I had only recently found it.

Dr Lestrange wagged an admonitory finger at me. 'Na, na, na,' he said. 'That won't do at all. We shan't get anywhere unless you are entirely open with me. People can turn up by chance, like the lady did last week. They see the plaque, wander in . . . Hypochondriacs mostly, attracted by the 'Dr' and the letters after my name. But people *like yourself* – he placed very strong emphasis on the last two words – 'no, they can't turn up by chance. They come because they have to, because they have run out of road. They have reached the T-junction, so to speak.' And he made a T with his hands, raised the flat one to eye level and squinted at me across its back, 'Is that not so? And they need a little push right or a little push left, whichever. Is that not so too? And sometimes – I might say, nearly always – they need a few guidelines first.'

I nodded hard. Guidelines at this point would be very welcome.

'Good. Let me explain to you, then. The service we provide is comprehensive: we offer counselling beforehand, we furnish means to effect the crossing, and we carry out whatever tidying-up operations are necessary afterwards. All technically free of charge, but . . . ' He sighed. 'Well, with the wolf population dwindling at the rate it is, and nearly everyone nowadays plumping for the human option, it's becoming increasingly difficult to conduct things in a discreet, convincing manner. Hence increasingly expensive too. You can't just leave your wolf carcass lying around anywhere, not in this country at any rate; you have to be prepared to travel. But anyway, we'll come to that later. At present we're still in phase one, are we not, and in the very early stages of that? So?' He leant back in his chair and steepled his fingers again. His boredom was very evident. 'How do things stand with you? Which is it to be? Wolf or woman? Any idea? Any particular leaning? Any clear preference?' It wouldn't have surprised me had he finished up with a yawn.

I'd been having trouble from the outset following the track of this bizarre conversation, but at last I got a feeling I was beginning to understand – at any rate the essentials. I didn't dare spell them out to myself, in case I was wrong, but a host of possibilities started buzzing around in my head – crazily, abortively, like flies in a bottle. Maybe, then, Nico . . . ? Maybe she didn't really . . . ? Maybe she still . . . somewhere . . . somehow . . . in some form or other . . . ? And maybe I can . . . ? 'You mean,' I said slowly, 'You mean I can choose whether I want to be a wolf in future or to go on being what I am?'

'Tch, tch, tch.' Dr Lestrange clicked his tongue in annoyance. 'Not what you *are*,' he said. 'That would be most foolish; that is exactly the problem we are here to resolve. At present you are a hapless halfway creature – that is the source of your discomfort, no? Exactly. No, the choice is between becoming a genuine hundred per cent wolf or a genuine hundred percent human being.'

I opened my mouth, more for oxygen than because I had anything to say, but the plump hand went up again, warning me to silence. 'Attention, though,' Dr Lestrange went on. 'Think it through very carefully before giving me your answer. You can leave now if you like, go home, mull it over, and come back in a week – in a month, in a year, whenever you feel ready. There is no hurry for you to arrive at a decision, provided in the end it is the right one. Because the step, once taken, is irreversible. Irreversible, you understand? I trust I make myself quite clear on this point: there is No Going Back, No "Sorry Dr Lestrange, I made a mistake, could you give me another potion." There *is* no other potion, there is only this one here. One single dose per capita per lifetime; one single administration.' And he rummaged in the drawer of his desk and took out a little brown bottle, which he waved in front of my nose and then replaced in the drawer again. 'However,' he added, 'for counselling purposes it is always helpful to know a client's initial inclination. So, at present, which way, if either, do you list?'

Hardly thanks to him, but at this point the pieces of jigsaw puzzle that the doctor had been tossing in my direction suddenly fitted together: I was in a sorting-house for werewolves, where Nico had been before me, and like her I was being offered the opportunity of healing my split condition by going either one way or the other, using some strange but evidently effective medicinal technique. Maybe it was naïve of me, but the thought that I might have fallen into the hands of an unscrupulous quack never entered my head. What entered it instead was peace. Peace and sunshine. It all made sense: Nico had not committed suicide, of course she hadn't, she had simply come here, made her choice, carried out her preparations and then gone over – gone over to the wolves. And for their sake she had tried to take with her as much knowledge as she could. Because that, I could see now, was the reason behind her passion for learning: she wanted to be of use to her new companions, help them in their every day harder struggle for survival. Astronomy, medicine, geography, natural history – at the time these had seemed to me rather an arbitrary selection of topics for her to concentrate on, but they weren't, not at all. On the contrary: the world, the stars, animal behaviour, sickness and how to heal it – they were a good solid pragmatic choice. Only music and poetry seemed, in retrospect, a little strange. What need was there in the forest for all that Bach and Shakespeare? How could the head of a wolf benefit from having those sounds and word patterns inside its skull? Well, no doubt I'd soon find out.

I was so absorbed by these thoughts, I had almost forgotten about Dr Lestrange – that I was sitting there in his consulting room, taking up his time, and that he was sitting opposite me, grudging it me and waiting for my answer. The drumming of his fingers on the desk brought me sharply back to the matter in hand. I did think it mightily inconsiderate of him, I must say, to show impatience in what, for me, was such a crucial moment. But then doctors get like that with time: they get hardened, their feelings get blunted.

It was therefore in quite a small, apologetic voice that

I announced my choice. Momentous to me, but to him probably just another string of chores to be dealt with – difficult, expensive chores, as he had so tactfully pointed out. 'Wolf,' I said. And then, because at this I saw him cup his hand behind his ear as if he hadn't heard me right, 'Wolf,' again, slightly louder. And finally, seeing that the word still didn't seem to catch his attention but that, on the contrary, he was now engrossed in a big mop-up job on his glasses: removing them and polishing them with a hanky and dabbing at his eyes as well, a third 'WOLF!' this time practically in a shout.

*   *   *

So there you are, Angie. Yes, because all I have written here is for you really. Story, explanation, apology and farewell – all for you. I don't want to run the risk Nico did and leave you a scrap of tissue paper you may not even find: I want you to have pages and pages that stacked together are as thick as a book. You won't have seen me for weeks when you receive them, maybe even for months – depending on when Dr Lestrange gets his act together and gives me the go-ahead – but when you do, and once you've read them, I know you will understand and forgive.

Don't be sad for me, not for a second. Don't even get emotional the way Doctor Lestrange himself did. (And by the way, don't go looking for him either: name and address are both fake.) Because I was wrong about him not listening or paying attention to my announcement: those were tears he was dabbing at with his hanky in the end. In his job he's impartial, but secretly he's on the side of the wild creatures, you see, and the surprise nature of my choice touched the heart inside his bureaucratic breast. He got very fatherly with me after that, pointed out all the drawbacks – the shortened life span, the harshness of conditions, the shrinking habitat and so forth – made a list of the things I would be renouncing, almost begged me for my own sake to change my mind and go human after all. And when he saw how set I was on the wolf option, and how anxious to be off, he came round to my side of the desk and almost hugged me, he was so moved.

Not *that* moved, mind you, that he didn't take my contribution to the fund or organization or whatever it is he belongs to, and pocket it fairly smartly. But, as he said himself, it's in a good cause and business is business, and there's also the cost of the plane ticket to Italy to consider. I wasn't quite sure what to give him, having so little money of my own, but then I remembered Nico's ring and gave him that, and he seemed very pleased, as indeed he should be. If he takes my tip and offers to sell it back again to the Sherwood estate he should raise a pretty good sum.

Am I nervous? Of course I am. I will have to jump off that towering great bridge, Angie, and you know how much I hate heights. I couldn't even reach down the cornflakes from the top shelf using a stool, remember? You had to do it for me. But don't worry, there's no pain involved, no hardship at all. Dr Lestrange has explained everything to me and told me exactly what I have to do. I have to take off all tight articles of dress, like watch, necklace, bracelet, rings etc – anything that might hamper me later in my new state, even pants and bra to make sure. Then once I've done that I down the potion, and almost immediately I shall find myself for a few bewildering seconds in both conditions: wolf and human. This, according to the doc, is the only tricky part where things can – theoretically, at any rate – go wrong, because actually *being* both things, and not having an outsider's view of the situation, only a double insider's, it's a little hard to know which 'I' is the one that has to jump and which remain. His solution in my case, which he says works perfectly well provided you don't lose both your heads and panic, is to have a red object of some kind handy, and to grab hold of it and not let go until you have taken the final step. Wolves don't see red apparently, so this – the sight of a red object – enables you to discern between your two selves.

Nico took a book: the Blake volume she had with her was bright vermillion, so that explains that. I think I will just buy some nail varnish and paint my fingernails. I needn't worry about it looking strange on my claws afterwards: Fuchsia Flame will be way outside the wolf spectrum. So too will the stain from the red inkpot. No more shame ever.

I will miss a lot, you say. Of course I will. I will miss you, Angie, for a start. And I will miss . . .

Oh, god, I can't even bear to make the list. And yet I have to go. I want to; there is nothing I want more. I can see us one evening, Nico and me, crossing a high hilltop and picking up with our sensitive ears the strains of some strange but compelling sound coming from the human settlement far below: festival time has come round again and in the square a pianist is playing Schubert's sonata – the special one that meant so much to us. We sit there on our haunches, our heads tilted to one side, listening, listening. Rapt; our wolf brains processing the material, perhaps remembering. Then slowly we turn to face each other. This is – was – music, man's sovereign achievement. Did we make the right choice?

In my case a little bubble of doubt may even surface – plimp! – rippling my tranquillity. But then I shall see Nico give a shrug of her high set shoulder blades, as much as to say, So what? We wolves have music too. And together we will throw back our heads and break into a snatch of song, just to show our bravura, before we trot happily back to the woods where we belong.

P.S. You will also find in the same parcel the little bag of Brazilian aquamarines. I offered to give them back to William, but all he said was, Fuck the fucking aquamarines, so I reckon I can do with them what I like, and what I like is that you have them made into a necklace and clasp them round your dear brown neck. They will look beautiful there. To quote William again in a gentler vein: think kindly of me sometimes, won't you, when you wear them.   S.